THE
CONFESSION

BY

PAT SIMMONS

Edited by Jo Davis
Proofread by Rahab Mugwanja
Beta Reader: Stacey Jefferson
Cover design: Nat/Bookaholic Fiverr.com
Author photo: Angie Knost Photography

ISBN-13: 978-1517624927
ISBN-10: 1517624924

Praise for Pat Simmons Novels:

Special thanks to

Dr. John Aden, Executive Director, African/African American Historical Society & Museum of Allen County, Ft. Wayne, Indiana

Mrs. Peggy Montes, Founder and Museum Chief Executive, Bronzeville Children's Museum, Chicago, Illinois

As always, I want to thank my readers and bookstores for supporting my work. A special shout-out to family and friends who let me know they are proud of me and praying for me.

A special hug and kisses to my husband—poor thing. He has to suffer through all my writing as I build the story, tweak the story, then finish rewrites on the story before the readers even see it. I appreciate you. I know the life of a writer's husband isn't easy, but I appreciate the healthy dinners you prepared and the kitchen you keep clean. Thank God for a good man— Kerry Simmons!

Prologue

"Babe, I think your mom needs a man in her life for companionship."

Kevin "Kidd" Jamieson was half-listening to his wife as they reclined on the back deck of their Suburban North St. Louis County home. They kept a watchful eye on their two-year-old daughter, Kennedy, who just discovered her shadow. Now, their toddler was running in circles trying to outsmart it.

Once Eva's words registered, Kidd angled his head and squinted at her angelic face that seemed to transform into an alien before him. "Huh?" He blinked to verify that it was indeed Eva Jamieson, then smirked. "Sweetheart, that's not possible. She has two beautiful granddaughters who adore her, with another grandbaby on the way." He grinned mischievously and reached over to massage her baby bump. She was about to begin her second trimester.

Eva's lids fluttered as she cooed from his massage. It was sensual watching her as he reverently touched her stomach. Clearly this second pregnancy was making her hormonal in ways he hadn't expected. First, since she'd received her license as an RN, she wanted to return to work after this baby was born, because she loved the residents. As a resident liaison at the same upscale nursing facility, Garden Chateau, he earned more than enough money to take care of his family.

Now she was talking nonsense about his aging mother in ways Kidd could only describe as creepy. Sandra Nicholson didn't need a man. She had two sons at her beck and call, but she rarely called. "Plus, Ma has two sons and two lovely daughters-in-law. How can she be lonely with that much love?"

Eva rolled her eyes, then dispatched "the look": a lifted eyebrow, jutted chin, and steely gaze. Kidd knew the signs. He had tangoed with these symptoms before. His wife of almost four years had a strong-willed personality that complemented his, but she wouldn't sway him on this. She swatted his hand away and scooted up in the lounger. "Would you stop thinking like an overbearing son? Our daughter and niece can only give their Nani so much attention." She lowered her voice to a seductive tease. "She needs the love of a good man, kissing, snuggling—"

"Hold it!" Scowling, Kidd shivered at the thought. She seemed to get a kick out of making him uncomfortable. "Stop it right there. This is my mother you're talking about—the same woman who insists on keeping her granddaughters on the weekends, so that her sons and their wives, who are in their early *thirties*, can have date nights," he reasoned before he spied Kennedy hurrying their way with a flower she picked from the spring garden Eva recently planted.

A daddy's girl, Kennedy could do no wrong. She was beautiful like her mother and generous with hugs and kisses. What more could a man ask for? His life was perfect. "Don't worry about Mom. She is probably somewhere using her

AARP card as we speak." Getting to his feet, Kidd brushed a kiss against his wife's forehead before meeting his daughter halfway.

Although Kidd considered his mother pretty and able to turn any man's eye, he did recently notice a silver strand—proof she was beyond her dating years. With his sister-in-law as the family's cosmetologist, Talise effortlessly managed to camouflage Mom's gray under her brown hair. No doubt, Sandra Nicholson was getting closer to senior citizen status. In fact, Kidd was sure that a love connection was the furthest thing from her mind.

On more than one occasion she had pretty much told him and his younger brother, Ace, that growing up. "I've had enough memories of my first love to last a lifetime." She hadn't meant it as a compliment. "I'm done." That seemed reason enough for her to be a homebody when not at church or work.

Getting to her feet, she rubbed her stomach, but didn't leave the deck. "Listen, Kidd—" Eva only used his nickname when she thought he was being stubborn, "—your mother is barely fifty-three years old. She *is* the new forty. If Beyoncé's mother, Tina Knowles, can be hot at sixty-one and remarry, don't you think your mother needs companionship too?"

Kidd's heart pricked. Sad to think that his mother had never married, so getting remarried wasn't an option. "She has a dog we gave her when she relocated here from Boston, remember?" He scooped up their daughter. "Sweetheart, please don't put any ideas in her head. Believe me, she's content." When she pouted, reminding him of Kennedy, he smirked.

His word was final—and he hoped Eva wouldn't try to

cook up some scheme to follow through with her concern. No doubt she would enlist assistance from the other Jamieson wives to carry out her mischief.

If she did go against his wishes, he and Ace were in trouble.

Chapter

One

"Excuse me." The richness of a baritone voice interrupted Sandra Nicholson's next sip of java as she stared out the window at the Nook Café. Glancing over her shoulder, Sandra expected to see... Well, she didn't know what she expected, but the good-looking gentleman with defined features wasn't it.

The mesmerizing voice matched a captivating man. *Wow*, she thought to herself as he seemed to study her.

"You are one incredibly beautiful woman," he stated as he towered over the table she shared with her son, who had minutes earlier excused himself to the men's room.

The stranger's timing couldn't have been more precise. A snarl from her overbearing son, and the man surely would have thought twice about stopping. What was taking Kidd so long, anyway?

Without waiting for her response, the distinguished gentleman swaggered out of Nordstrom's boutique café and disappeared into the store, leaving a trail of his designer cologne as his calling card. His stride had been as confident as his declaration.

Sandra did her best not to ogle, but she conducted a quick assessment in less than sixty seconds. She guessed him to be about six-one or two and would tower over her five-seven frame. Judging from his wavy thick salt-and-pepper curly hair that complemented his brown skin, the man was in his late forties, early fifties. If good genes ran in his family, he could have been hovering over eighty for all she knew. Yet, his confident stride hinted of a man who was youthful and fit. With jaw-dropping looks, she pegged him as a ladies man in his heyday, or even now. Sandra knew how to call them, because she had been charmed by the top-of-the-line Samuel Jamieson. She dismissed the temptation at the same time Kidd reappeared, talking on his cell phone.

"Eva," he mouthed.

She nodded as he took his seat, then her mind drifted once again to the striking stranger. It wasn't like she didn't receive compliments here and there, but it was the commanding way he said it that made her want to pass out and never regain consciousness if it meant he would be in her dreams. Because he said it, Sandra felt beautiful. Maybe it was the highlights in her hair that her daughter-in-law, Talise, insisted she try or maybe it was the ensemble she had meticulously assembled to wear.

"Okay, babe. Don't worry. I'm on my way." Lines etched Kidd's forehead, which put Sandra on alert. No time for whimsical musing as she leaned forward with concern. "Is everything okay?"

"No." He gritted his teeth. "The car won't start and

6

Kennedy has a doctor's appointment. Sorry, Mom, we have to cut our breakfast date short." He stood and pulled a twenty out his wallet then kissed her cheek. "Are you going to be all right?"

Sandra smiled. "No apologies needed, son. Go see about my grandbaby. She's your priority."

"But you're right up there at the top of my list too." Snatching his jacket off the back of his chair, he hurried off.

The monthly breakfast treat was her older son's idea for some one-on-one time. Even though he was married, he still felt obligated to look after her as if she was an ailing out-of-shape granny in her eighties, not a woman who had yet to experience a hot flash.

In her mid-50s, Sandra had regrets in her life. One, she had yet to marry. Even after she repented of her deeds and accepted the salvation outlined in the Book of Acts, God hadn't blessed her in that way. Second, the man who fathered her two sons out of wedlock wasn't worth the heartache he caused her. But the Lord had given her two beautiful granddaughters to spoil—one from each son. And she did without any guilt trips from their scolding.

As a personal fashion consultant and shopper, Sandra set her own schedule. She didn't have to meet with her client until this afternoon. She had worked in the insurance industry for most of her adult life to provide for her boys. With her 401K and pension, Sandra had quit her job in Boston and relocated to St. Louis to be closer to family. That move seemed to liberate her and she explored her creative side. She was finally, after thirty years, putting her fashion merchandising degree to work.

Sandra glanced around the café. No other male patron

seemed to pay her any mind. She didn't consider herself vain. She strived to live with a humble spirit, but a male compliment, not coming from her sons, did make her smile. *Wait until I tell the Jamieson girls about this.* She chuckled as she finished her crepes and fruit.

I can't believe what I just said. Raimond Mayfield snickered, amused by his actions, but he had no regrets. He had told the truth.

It was as if God was his dining partner and had turned his head in the direction of that beautiful woman. But his womanizing days were long gone and God had his record when he repented of his past sins.

Yet, the Lord seemed to push him out of his seat, because he wasn't moving fast enough. Once Raimond began his trek, there was no turning back.

Somehow Raimond managed to sneak a peek at her hands. All fingers were void of jewelry. Her beauty so empowered him that he briefly thought about inviting himself to join her. But he saw another plate and her dining companion was missing, so he decided to keep going. In hindsight, he should have stuck around and introduced himself, if for no other reason, on a professional level as curator of the new Black museum.

He walked aimlessly through the men's clothing section, but his mind was still in the café. Raimond couldn't shake the natural glow from her face when she turned around. His eyes seemed to zoom in on her features like a microscope. The small curve of her cheeks seemed to be positioned to be cupped by a man's hands. Her hair framed her face and her brown eyes brightened when they met his. Her lips puckered, but nothing came out. Yes, God had formed a masterpiece. Raimond was no stranger to beauties; he had married one. Later, they divorced, to no fault of his ex-wife, but his. Then for years, Raimond enjoyed the endless selection in the dating pool. That was, until Jesus commandeered his soul and he had repented shamefully before he was baptized with water and fire in Jesus' name. God had truly become his heart regulator.

So what happened back there? Raimond had just concluded an early morning business meeting with a senior manager in one of the departments at Nordstrom. The potential backer's interest was piqued by Raimond's theme for The Heritage House. His mind switched back to his sweet tooth, in the form of a woman and not a pastry on the shelf.

Raimond felt like a giddy teenager rather than a seasoned adult. Banishing all thoughts of the woman, he browsed through the shirts selection. "Lord, why did You have me make a fool out of myself?" he mumbled as he grabbed three shirts then stepped over the rack of ties.

Suddenly, he experienced an unexplainable sensation that ran down his back. Then the soft melodious female voice spoke from behind him.

"Pick the lilac shirt and that yellow and lilac print tie." The same beautiful woman came to his side. He was speechless as her lips puckered, as if she was contemplating his purchase as her own. "Get the lilac and yellow paisley. It goes good with your skin tone."

With the wave of her hand, she strutted away in a dress that outlined her figure, and all Raimond could do was stare with his jaw slacked. *God, did You do that?*

Once he closed his mouth and breathed, Raimond acted

like an obedient student. He checked the shirt's neck size and grabbed the tie the beauty queen had suggested, then he sought out a clerk to ring his purchase.

Twice their paths had crossed—two times, he repeated looking at his fingers. He didn't believe in coincidences. "Lord, if You give me one more chance today, I'll take it as a sign to properly introduce myself and get her number." Next time, *if* there was a next time, Raimond wouldn't be tongue-tied again.

The clerk greeted him and accepted his merchandise. After verifying the sale price and changing the register tape, the transaction was complete. The young man handed Raimond the bag with a smile. "Thanks for shopping at Nordstrom. Enjoy your day."

Not without seeing that woman again, I won't, Raimond thought. He trekked to the women's department, then the perfume counters, but there was no sign of the lady in orange, peach, or whatever the shade she was wearing. He huffed and did another sweep of the store, which wasn't crowded. *Gone.*

Heading to the parking lot, Raimond chalked it up to a missed opportunity. He strolled to his SUV, tossed his purchases in the back, and slid behind the wheel. While waiting at the light to exit the shopping plaza, he lowered his window to enjoy the freshness of spring. A flash of orange came into his peripheral vision at the same time the light changed to green, and he accelerated. He whipped his head around—it was "her."

He lost all manner of proper etiquette as he honked and yelled, "Excuse me, excuse me." He waved to get her attention. That's when Raimond slammed into the back of the car in front of him.

Chapter

Two

Shouting, then a crash, equaled road rage to Sandra's summation as she whipped her head around to see what happened. A black shiny SUV vs. a compact car was not good. When both drivers got out, there was something familiar about the man. *Wait a minute.* Sandra strained her eyes. Was that the suave gentleman from earlier who was involved? Was he the one yelling? Judging from his earlier coolness, she would've never pegged him as a road rager. So he was a jerk under nice clothing. However, he appeared calm now as the other driver, a young woman, became frantic after she assessed the damage.

Someone had to come to the girl's aide. Toned from morning runs and power walks, Sandra didn't skip a beat in her high heels. Within minutes she joined the growing number of bystanders. Sandra pushed her way through the crowd, ignored the handsome stranger, and directed her attention to the other motorist. "Are you okay?"

The driver nodded as a tear skipped down her cheeks. "My dad is going to kill me." Her voice trembled with fear.

Sandra took the liberty of rubbing the girl's back, who appeared to be in her early twenties, if that old. She asked her name as she eyed the back of the car. There was definitely some visual damage. Hopefully, the girl's death was an exaggeration.

"Sarah," she whispered. She blinked and released more tears.

The handsome gentleman apologized. "It was my fault, young lady." He reached for his wallet. "We can exchange driver's information while we wait for the police. I called them right away."

His tone had such a calming effect that even Sandra relaxed. Maybe she'd judged him too quickly. "I'll speak with your father, if that will help," he offered. His expression was gentle and his light brown eyes—that she just noticed—were filled with compassion, but they seemed to sparkle when he met her glance.

Two squad cars rolled to synchronized stops. One officer stepped out, a woman, and strolled their way, scrutinizing the damage before speaking. "If both vehicles are drivable, please pull to the side of the road," she instructed as the other officer directed traffic around them.

Since everything seemed under control, Sandra turned to head back to her car. "Please, don't go," he said with an underlying urgency.

Sandra looked around. Was he talking to her? She patted her chest. "Me?"

"Yes, please," he asked again, then climbed into his SUV that didn't appear to be scratched and parked it on the side of the road. Getting out, he answered the officer's questions. "Yes, it was my fault. I was distracted. I have an otherwise good driving record and insurance."

The policewoman nodded, took both their cards and went back to her patrol car. With Sarah on the phone, the man approached Sandra. "My name is Raimond with an 'i' Mayfield. I'll take one hundred percent blame for running into the back of her car, but you're the one hundred and one percent distraction that caused me to do it. I'm sorry for hanging out the window to get your attention. You didn't deserve that, but I don't know your name and I couldn't let you out of my sight again without knowing it."

A sprinkle of gray at his temples and the littering of silver in his goatee made him the distraction, so she could see that even a simple name had to be tweaked to describe him. And he was a classic flirt. "Sandra Nicholson."

His eyes seemed to twinkle. "Sandra, unless another man has been so blessed to call you his..." He paused. "Have lunch with me."

Blinking, she didn't know whether to be flattered or skeptical. "You're a reckless driver, which you admitted to quite readily. I'm sure that won't earn you bonus points with your insurance and now you're asking me out to lunch?"

"Yes." He nodded.

Honesty? She gave him kudos for that. Seemingly more handsome than he was less than an hour earlier, Sandra couldn't stop her lips from curling into a smile and then a giggle spilled out. She *was* flattered. This man was fresh with a zest of craziness, but somehow, he made her interested.

When the officer signaled for him, Raimond stared into her eyes. "Don't move."

"Another demand?" She lifted an eyebrow and crossed her arms.

"No, a pleading request." He matched her eyebrow lift with one of his thick silky ones, then he rejoined the officer and Sarah.

Just for the mystery, Sandra stayed. While he was distracted, she admired his broad shoulders. The fit and quality of his clothes—and his shoes—were stylish. Was she reckless for even considering his lunch proposal? She gnawed on her lips.

Minutes later, Raimond trekked back to her as the officers and Sarah got into their vehicles and drove off. "Do you have an answer for me, yet?" His smile was engaging.

Do I? Sandra asked herself as she jutted her chin. Yes was on the tip of her tongue, which she didn't say very often when a man asked her out. Being naïve once had a lasting effect on a woman. Samuel Jamieson was decades ago. Since her first love, she was no longer easily charmed. As he waited, it appeared patiently, for her answer, her heart and soul were in the midst of a tug of war. At that very moment, on that very day, with that man giving her a cute puppy dog expression, minus the pout, Sandra fantasized about being chased and captured. *Now where did that thought come from?*

"No." The word was hardly out before she wished she could retrieve it, so she had to stand by it.

His brown eyes danced with mischief as he reached inside his breast jacket pocket and whipped out a card. Had Raimond accepted her decision without a rebuttal? *I guess he didn't read my mental memo that I wanted to be chased!* As if his baritone voice wasn't mesmerizing enough, he lowered it to a Barry White whisper. "I stand by my compliment from

14

earlier and although I don't lack confidence, I was hesitant about approaching you." He looked bashful. "This might not make sense to you, but I felt as if the Lord wanted you to hear how beautiful you are to Him and me and I'm sure yours is more than outward. I walked away never expecting to see you again." His nostrils flared as he inhaled. "While I was in the men's department, I asked God to allow our paths to cross again." He smirked. "I didn't know it was going to cost me."

How endearing. "It does make sense to me," she assured him and relaxed, only for her mind to shout, *Stay on guard.* Sandra glanced at the card. "So you don't have a habit of flirting with women and you always admit your mistakes?" She tilted her head toward his vehicle.

"I've learned in my life that telling the truth will set me free from guilt."

God and guilt. What an interesting combination. Was it what he was saying or his voice that was melting her resolve as she slowly unfolded her arms and accepted his card? Smithsonian Institute was printed in bold letters across the top. *Research specialist* was listed under his uniquely spelled name. "So you're visiting?"

"No, I'm relocating." The wind stirred and Sandra got a whiff of his cologne. She liked that fragrance and had suggested it to a client. "So if you're not married, I would love to take you out to breakfast, lunch, and dinner."

"All of the above?" Sandra snickered in amusement. She shifted her legs in her heels as he nodded. "If you're *not* married, I'll think about it. Now, excuse me, I have some clients to meet." She turned to cross the street. Raimond startled her when he followed and strolled the short distance with her. Why did that gesture remind her of Samuel? She swallowed. Would she always be suspect of every male's attention and think he was like Ace and Kidd's father? A tiny voice answered, *Yes.* "I'm sure the police will come back if I call and report I'm being stalked."

"Once I explain that I was trying to get your number, they would understand." He slowed his stride to match hers.

Sandra stopped. "You didn't answer my question. Are you married?"

"No." Raimond didn't bat an eye.

"Can you prove it?" She challenged him. Silly question, but nothing about the day's events made any sense. This time, he broke eye contact. His confidence slipped into a crestfallen expression. "I have a divorce decree to prove it. I'm not proud of that, but I'm so glad to be forgiven."

Forgiveness. Sandra had firsthand experience with that. She felt bad for piercing his armor. "I'll think real hard, then."

"You do that, and I'll be praying even harder."

Minutes later, Sandra slid behind the wheel. She took a deep breath, held it, then exhaled slowly. "Lord, if you gave Raimond a word about me, do You have anything for me about him?" She turned off the radio and waited for His whisper.

God said nothing.

"There are standard protocols for picking up women, and wrecking a car in the process isn't one of them," Townsend Shaw hooted over the phone from his office at the Smithsonian in D.C.

Raimond grunted. Townsend was young enough to be the son he never had. On a business level, Raimond had mentored him as a protégé. On a personal level, Raimond had been the worst example of a man before Christ redeemed him. Yet, his friend had stayed in his corner during the good and bad times, displaying a genuine concern to earn his place as Raimond's confidant.

But their bond didn't keep Raimond from becoming annoyed as Townsend badgered him. "It was a fender bender, okay? That was simply a diversion from an otherwise memorable day. Besides meeting a beautiful woman, another businessman committed to funding for the museum's grand opening," he stated as he stretched his legs and rested them on one of several unpacked moving boxes. He had yet to tackle them, because of long hours at the museum or business breakfasts, brunches, luncheons, dinner, and anything else to drum up funding for The Heritage House. For months, he had used them as a makeshift ottoman, coffee table, and kitchen table.

"It was a day to remember all right, but I'm sure this Sandra lady will conveniently forget, because she's probably pegged you as crazy. My advice for next time is don't let there be a next time," he reprimanded.

Now who sounded like the father? Yet, his friend was right. Raimond could only focus on one woman at a time. Heading up The Heritage House Museum in St. Louis was just a cover for his true mission and only Townsend was privy to the real reason he had left Washington, D.C.—Kelsi.

As a senior consultant to hundreds of black museums across the country, Raimond knew what worked and what didn't. He had done the feasibility study on whether the St. Louis community would support another historic museum that would tell the stories buried, or rather forgotten, about Africans and African Americans in America.

He earnestly wanted to bring a slice of the Smithsonian's National Museum of African American History and Culture to St. Louis. Townsend assisted him in researching federal grants with the National Endowments for The Arts, Endowment for the Humanities, and other charitable agencies listed with the Foundation Center Online Directory.

If the Ford Motor Company could help fund the Charles II. Wright Museum of African American History in Detroit, then he hoped major St. Louis based corporations would be so generous, especially with the significance of an Underground Railroad station in the adjacent state of Illinois. Their effects had been exhausting, but worth it. But the local public support would have to sustain it.

Once the initial funding was secured, Raimond had to scout for the right location, which was key. Any street corner wouldn't do, if black museums were to thrive. The location had to be accessible for tourists and in a cultural district for locales.

After more than a year in preparation, Raimond couldn't wait any longer for the perfect time…

"You are so out of the game, Rai," Townsend said, pulling him from his musing. "That was a lot of trouble to get a woman's attention and now, it appears you're going to pay for it—big time."

Raimond sighed and glanced around his rental. He really needed to hang a picture or something, if he opted to call this place home. "Some things are worth the cost. Higher premiums are the least of my concerns."

"You haven't gotten the bill yet." Townsend cleared his throat. "Okay, so you had a minor distraction—"

"Major," Raimond argued.

"Right. Let's stay focused on Kelsi. You have too much riding on this second chance." He became quiet. "I hope she can see what I see—a better man. I'm pulling and praying for you my friend. As today proves, Sandra would be a diversion." He snickered. "Maybe that was the reason you made a fool out of yourself," he added before they said their goodbyes.

Kelsi. Raimond made another call to her that night before retiring. He was hopeful for a breakthrough, but Raimond got her voice mail—again and left a message—again. Anchoring his elbows on his knees, Raimond bowed his head and closed his eyes. "Jesus, I know You've forgiven me, but I need Kelsi's forgiveness too."

Surely, he could multitask and juggle two women in his life. "Right, Lord?"

God said nothing.

Chapter

Three

"Whew." Talise Jamieson wore a whimsical expression as she fanned herself. "Any man who would stop traffic for me is definitely worth a lunch date," the wife of Sandra's youngest son teased from her perch on the sofa in Sandra's bungalow.

"Raimond Mayfield has my vote." Eva grinned and lifted her hand in the air, reminding Sandra of a grade school pupil. "And you know Grandma BB would give her stamp of approval once he clears his background check."

Sandra's relationship with her daughters-in-law felt more like that of sister-girlfriends than the dreaded meddling mother-in-law. Sandra's social life definitely wasn't a typical Saturday afternoon conversation when her daughters-in-law came to pick up their little girls. Friday night sleepovers with her granddaughters were always the highlight of Sandra's weekends. Most times, their chats were centered on the toddlers.

Mrs. Beatrice Tilley Beacon, better known as Grandma

BB by all those who either loved or feared her, was a childless widow who carried a reputation as a woman not to be crossed or that it was in the best interest of others to let her have her way. Recalling previous antics of the "family matriarch," who wasn't blood kin to any Jamieson, caused the three of them to laugh, which triggered Lauren and Kennedy to scream their delight, thinking they were the center of attention.

It didn't take long for the little cousins to return to Sandra's Yorkie, Boston, who barked for the girls to toss him his toy. They did, then busied themselves with the dolls Sandra had just purchased for them. Although Kennedy was three months older, Lauren's feisty personality caused her cousin to cave in to her demands of treats and toys. Sandra spoiled them equally the same.

"Mom, your happiness has been a long time coming." Talise's eyes pleaded with Sandra to entertain the notion of a date.

Even though she was close with both daughters-in-law, who were both godly women, Sandra connected more with Talise. They both had found themselves young and pregnant by Jamieson men without the benefit of marriage.

Sandra had never insisted that either woman call her Mom, but her heart warmed with Talise's endearment, which usually resulted when she was passionately making a point. Sandra filled a yearning void since Talise's mother had died long before she met Ace.

With God's guidance, Sandra maintained impartiality as Talise's friend and mothered her through the pregnancy. She was there for Talise when Ace had lost his mind and turned his back on his then girlfriend. Then God laid a guilt trip on

Ace that had him begging Talise for another chance as a redeemed man who would practice Christian values to the end with the help of the Holy Ghost.

Then there was her first born. She smiled, thinking how Eva's strong-willed personality had brought Kidd's bull-headed self to his knees before God in repentance.

To Sandra's knowledge, Samuel had never repented and received God's salvation before he died, after fathering eleven children, most of them between two marriages. She never envisioned a happily ever after with a man that her daughters-in-law enjoyed.

"You're smiling," Eva teased in a singsong voice. "So does this mean you're thinking about Rai-Rai?"

"No," Sandra answered truthfully. She had ceased thinking about having a husband a long time ago.

Bored with their toys, the girls ran to their respective mothers. Sandra watched their tender interaction as Talise coaxed Lauren for a kiss and Kennedy climbed on Eva's lap for a hug before kissing her stomach.

Turning around, Lauren raced to Sandra and patted her lap. "Juice, Nani."

Kennedy dittoed the demand, so Sandra got up and took both their hands and led them to the kitchen. Away from Eva and Talise's watchful eyes, Sandra recounted their conversation. Both encouraged her to date, but Sandra wasn't sure.

As she handed Kennedy, then Lauren their sippy cups, Sandra smiled. When was the last time someone called her beautiful? And by a man so handsome that his looks would put a woman into a trance. Of course, her sons and wives complimented her many times on her pretty attire and a few clients, both male and female, had called her stunning but beautiful. Coming from Raimond's lips, Sandra felt like petals on a flower, opening up to enjoy the morning sun. She thought about Samuel again. The day she met him, it had rained. In hindsight, that had been an omen to run for higher ground.

When she and the girls returned to her living room, Eva and Talise ceased their whispered conversation and began to giggle. Finally, Talise spoke up. "Sandra, you don't need anyone's permission to live. You are beautiful as Raimond rightly said."

"Live the fantasy. Our girls need a grandpa." Eva winked, barely containing a fit of laughter.

"I'm not looking for a husband," Sandra said and squinted at Eva, "and the girls don't need a grandpa. They have daddies."

"But you need to be loved," Talise stated. That was something Sandra's lips wouldn't let her deny, so she said nothing.

Soon they switched subjects from the children to fashions to decoration until Kidd called first, then Ace, wanting their families to come home. Sandra received their goodbye hugs and kisses. As she closed the door behind them, Sandra felt an unexplainable loss that she never experienced before. She dismissed it as she put away the girls' toys until next time. Her life was fine just the way it was.

Hours later, as Sandra prepared for bed, she scanned Raimond's business card again. She had no words to describe Raimond except a mysterious temptation. She hadn't resisted temptation when she met Samuel and like Adam and Eve when they yielded, her life was changed forever.

Raimond drummed his fingers on the table as he waited at Cardwell's at the Plaza. He had roses for Sandra for whenever she arrived. He didn't care that it took her four and a half days to call and then another three days for their schedules to align. His heart pounded in anticipation of seeing her again. Of course, Townsend's warning voice about getting distracted nagged at him, but there was something about Sandra's attraction that made him forget everything.

Yes, he hadn't lost sight of the mission to reconcile with the woman who drew him back to St. Louis, but Sandra dominated his thoughts and he entertained them instead of rejecting them.

Raimond had left the site of the future museum in the hands of volunteers who were assisting in phase one of getting the building ready for a Juneteenth opening. He'd visited a barber before heading home to shower and change out of one business suit to the gray one, which would boast the tie Sandra had suggested with the shirt.

With his eyes trained on the entrance, Raimond smiled the moment Sandra came into view. Everything else paled as she exited a store in the adjacent Plaza Frontenac mall. Raimond indulged in a bold assessment of a woman who could stop a church offering.

Then Raimond noticed a male companion, who walked in sync alongside Sandra as if they had rehearsed a routine, so he stood. With a ready smile, he started to meet her halfway. Another man was never his competition. Plus, he looked too old for her to be a serious contender.

"Hi." His simple greeting made her blush, of which

Raimond did a mental screen shot for later. As he drew her into his gaze, Raimond hoped he was shutting out the world. Unfortunately, her sidekick didn't have a problem with three being a crowd. Raimond gave him a pointed look. "And you are?" he asked when it appeared an introduction was taking too long.

"This is my client, Mr. Lawson," Sandra stated.

"I'm Raimond Mayfield." Raimond made sure he mustered a smile to be cordial as they shook hands and prayed this man wouldn't be joining them. "Well, it *was* nice meeting you," he said, putting the emphasis on the past tense.

"Same here." The man nodded and stepped back, then faced Sandra. "Thanks for the suggestion about the jewelry. I'm sure my sweetheart will like it. Enjoy your dinner."

"Thanks, we will." He guided her to their table.

Unlike the first time he saw her, her sandy brown hair was straight, which made her more youthful, and the dress accented her figure. This woman was the complete package, physically. He was eager to find out how they complemented each other's interest. Once she took her seat, Raimond handed her the flowers, then took his seat across from her. "For you."

Sandra's eyes brightened and she accepted the half-dozen orange roses.

As if cued, their server appeared with menus, introduced himself, took their drink orders, then left them alone. While she admired the flowers, he admired her. Sandra had soft, delicate features and her lips were the focal point. Upon further inspection, Raimond couldn't tell if the Lord had outlined her eyes, or if it was a trick of a makeup artist's eyeliner. Whichever was the case, Raimond approved.

When Sandra looked up and caught him staring, Raimond

felt no shame. "So, Miss Nicholson, how many men's eyes did you catch today?" He chuckled.

She shrugged. "I hope all of them," she stated in a cool manner, then reached for her glass of lemonade the server placed before her.

"Huh?" He blinked, not expecting that comeback. Was she high-maintenance? "I mean, pardon me?"

She gave him a mischievous smile, showcasing stain-free white teeth. "I'm a fashion personal shopper. My job is to catch everyone's eye."

Raimond exhaled. *Good answer*, he silently cheered as if he was playing *Family Feud*; a woman with confidence and the flair to dress others. He liked that, although he was clueless what that profession entitled. "How can I go about hiring you as my personal shopper?"

"With a MasterCard, Visa, American Express, Discover, or a check. We'll make an appointment for me to do a profile of your activities, favorite colors, and the image you want to portray."

Mentally adding great personality to her profile, Raimond flirted. "Whatever image will impress you."

Sandra lifted an eyebrow and twisted her lips. "The only thing that impresses me from a man is honesty."

Raimond sensed an underlining warning in her tone. He dismissed it, since he had nothing to hide. "Like when I said you were the prettiest woman I've ever seen." His nostrils flared.

"Am I no longer beautiful?" she teased and they both laughed.

Their server reappeared and both scrambled to pick up their menus and place an order. Once they did, the man left to do their bidding.

"For a moment, I thought Mr. Lawson was joining us for dinner."

She released a melodious laugh. "I'm sure he would have, if I wanted him to. I did ask him to follow me, because I was meeting a blind date."

Raimond frowned. "I wouldn't exactly call this a blind date." He straightened his body. "You're too memorable for me to forget and I hope I was the same."

"True, but it never hurts for someone to see who you're meeting. Otherwise, I'm not worried, because I can knock a man unconscious, using my self-defense skills."

Raimond roared with uncontrollable laughter. "You won't have to worry about defending yourself against me. I've never laid a hand on a woman."

"That's good to know, because physically, you'd be requesting a death sentence from my sons after you regain consciousness." She didn't smile.

"I have been warned." Folding his hands, Raimond sobered. "Seriously, how did you get into becoming a fashion personal shopper?"

"The short answer is I graduated from Bay State College in Boston in the eighties with a bachelor of arts in fashion merchandising. I was offered a perk job at Saks headquarters in New York." A flash of sadness filled Sandra's eyes, then it faded away. "But I took a detour. My priorities changed when I had two sons that I never pursued my passion while I reared them. Both are married now and made me a doting Nani." Sandra's eyes sparkled before she smiled.

While some people talked with their hands, Sandra's eyes spoke volumes. "I still love fashion and how it's displayed, whether on people or in a window. At this point in my life, I don't want to be confined, so freelancing as a fashion personal shopper allows me the flexibility to be at the beck and call of my granddaughters." Her eyes lit up again.

He nodded. Raimond envied how her life had come full circle for her to be happy, despite those detours. He also admired her strengths. "So what exactly do you do, besides spending people's money?" he teased.

She playfully squinted. It was a flirtatious gesture. "I'm a visual person. While one customer may see a roomful of shoes, shelves full of hats and racks of clothes, I envision colors, styles, and accents, then I put them together in a complete ensemble. Sometimes, I meet with clients to advise them on purchases. Recently, I had to give my opinion on a piece of jewelry that would complement a woman's personality. Other times, I do the shopping for them. I'm cost conscious to work with any budget, from a stay-at-home mother returning to the work force, someone attending a gala, or clients wanting to update their wardrobe."

"Which explains…" He cataloged everything about her— color choice, accessories. She wore a badge of fashion. "Why you brightened my day."

"Thank you." Sandra lowered her lashes as she blushed.

When she looked up at him, Raimond swallowed. The woman was breathtaking, and he didn't mind piling on the compliments, but he wanted to know more about her. He picked at his napkins when it was apparent she was waiting on him to say something. Leaning back, he stretched out his legs and lightly brushed hers. She shifted in her seat. "I thought I detected an East Coast dialect."

She gave him a mock salute and jutted her chin in pride. "Boston born and reared. I lived there until my sons moved here, and I followed them a year later."

When their meals arrived, Raimond took the opportunity to wrap her hands in his as he said grace. They were soft, but they also were conjuring up carnal desires.

Yield to Me for a man can't serve two masters, God whispered. *Have you not read Matthew 6:24?*

Raimond's heart was immediately pricked. Clearing his head, he wasted no time repenting. "Father, in the name of Jesus, we thank You for Your mercy and grace. Please sanctify this meal, help us to give to those who are hungry, and bless our fellowship. In Jesus' name…" She joined him in uttering, "Amen."

While eating, Raimond found it a struggle to dismiss Sandra's beauty, but he was determined to bind every temptation about her for God's glory. Shying away from further compliments, he stayed with safe topics. "Okay, since this is a first date, I have to ask you your favorite color, hobbies, middle name…"

She tilted her head and seemed to study him. "Pinks, purples, shades of red." She laughed. "It's hard to pick just one color. I like to shop for a hobby, but you would've never guessed that."

He grinned. "Never."

"Speaking of colors, not every man could pull off wearing purple, but that tie just seems…" her eyes wandered as if she was searching for the right description, "…to prove your confidence."

About time she noticed the tie, he thought. He grinned. "Thank you."

"And my middle name is Lynette." Sandra pushed aside her plate and rested her arms on the table. "Enough about me.

What about you? With a job at the Smithsonian, what brings you to St. Louis?"

He pinched his napkin before answering. "My ex-wife." If Sandra's eyes could change color, Raimond was sure he would be seeing black. The blank expression on her face put Raimond on alert to look out for one of her self-defense moves. But he had no games to play. They both believed in honesty.

Chapter

Four

Not again, Sandra thought, blinking to keep her eyes from tearing. She refused to be the mistress in another relationship. Whereas Samuel Jamieson had omitted that he was married when they first met, and she was too enthralled to ask, Raimond was laying his cards on the table to see if she wanted to play the game. *The man is divorced, yet he's running back to his ex-wife?*

Leaning closer, she lowered her voice. "Not that I'm proud of my past before Christ, but I've been the other woman, Raimond. History will not repeat itself with me." She gathered her purse and made a move to stand. She was out of there.

"I have a past too, before Christ saved me with His blood."

Be quick to hear, but slow to anger, God reminded her of James 1:19.

Sandra took a deep breath and released her purse. God wanted her to listen. "Go on."

Raimond nodded. "Thank you." His baritone voice seemed to drop lower. "My ex-wife remarried three years after I cut out on her and our daughter—I'm not proud of my behavior." He squeezed his lips as if he had a bitter taste in his mouth.

Sandra couldn't stop her heart from sinking. She knew about abandonment and she hadn't been married.

Don't judge him for his past sins, God whispered. *I forgave him as I have forgiven you.*

Help me, Lord, not to, she silently prayed.

"I found out my daughter got married five years ago and her stepfather walked her down the aisle. Now she's having a baby." He grunted and twisted his lips in disgust or regret. Sandra couldn't tell. "What did I expect? I don't know why that hurt, but it did something to me." Raimond patted his chest. "That was the turning point in my life when I accepted I had failed as a human being. God started to deal with me. Without any way to reach Kelsi, I had no choice but to go through my ex-wife and you can't imagine the hate she spewed at me, with just cause. She released a truckload of all my sins."

"I can," she mumbled and was glad Raimond didn't hear her or ignored her.

"I withstood Ivy's darts of fire for the sake of Kelsi. Ivy dared me that if I was serious, I'd pack up and move back to St. Louis. It wasn't *that* easy, but after praying hard and working harder toward that mission, I'm opening The Heritage House, a new black History museum here. Failure isn't an option financially, or here." He placed his hand over his heart, then gave a dry chuckle.

"It's funny. My background is about historic preservation,

making sure documents are handled a particular way, stored in a certain climate control environment, and labeling artifacts... Yet, I didn't preserve or cherish the important things in my own life." He rested his hand on the table.

As Sandra witnessed the tortured expression on Raimond's otherwise smug face, her heart ached for him. She placed her hand on top of his. It was stiff at first then he relaxed.

The server reappeared and offered dessert choices, but Sandra's appetite was to learn more about the man who had a strong exterior, but seemed broken inside. "From the beginning, tell me what happened?"

Raimond seemed uncomfortable as he loosened his tie—ties were her favorite men's garment, because the right tie did make the man. But her mind was getting sidetracked. She refocused as he glanced around the restaurant before meeting her eyes again. "I was twenty-three when Ivy and I married. Within a year, she was pregnant. I thought I loved Ivy. I say *thought* because I never learned the responsibility that came with love." His proud shoulders slumped in defeat.

"The old Raimond didn't want that burden. After I cheated once, each time it got easier. Ivy confronted me and I didn't deny it. I was glowing with sin. I wanted to be free of any entanglements, so I moved out, despising my wife and resenting my child. I was wretched."

Hmmm-mm. Sandra agreed with him. As a matter of fact, she wanted to deliver some blows on behalf of his ex-wife.

"We divorced. I moved to D.C. where I continued my ways until God let me know that payday was coming and the seeds I sowed weren't fruitful, and hell was ready to receive me in torment." He shook his head as if in disbelief. "After I confessed every thought and deed I could think of, I'll never forget the sermon Bishop E. Jefferson preached in D.C. about one of the biggest deceptions Satan uses to make us believe our sins aren't as bad as someone else's, and if you don't bother me with mine, I won't bother you with yours. When he finished, stating that all unrighteousness is sin that earns some type of severe punishment, the eyes to my soul seemed to pry open."

Without realizing it, moisture had blurred Sandra's vision as if she could smell the sweet fragrance of his testimony. For the briefest moment she hoped Samuel had repented like that and she just wasn't privy to it? Despite how their relationship turned out, she didn't want Samuel to spend eternity in hell.

"I can't get back the years I stole from Kelsi as a father, but I'm praying that God will open her heart and she'll allow me to be a grandpa to her child."

"Oh, Raimond." Sandra wanted to kiss and make it better as she had done to her sons growing up. "I'll be praying for the same, because there is nothing like getting a second chance at being a role model and bonding with your only child."

Raimond looked away, but not before Sandra glimpsed a hint of moisture in his eyes. She waited as he gathered his thoughts.

"I hadn't planned to say all that, but as I told you on the day of the accident, I've learned from my past experience to be truthful and accept responsibility, so… I'm hoping maybe I haven't scared you off and you'll pencil me into your schedule on a personal and professional level."

His testimony had given her a change of heart just like she had a change of heart to call and accept his dinner invitation after steadfastly refusing to entertain such a thing. Maybe that was God nudging her to befriend him. "I would like that."

His confidence seemed to bounce back before her eyes. The crooked smile he gave her made Sandra blush, which was okay with her, as she eyed his tie again. It really was a good choice with his suit.

"So you know about my passion. Tell me about yours?" She didn't have to meet with a client until the next day midmorning, so she wasn't in a rush to leave. "Why a black history museum?"

"Why not? Forty out of fifty states have some type of African American cultural center or museum in their major cities. At last count, there are one hundred and seventy."

Sandra blinked, flabbergasted. She didn't know what to say.

Raimond grinned. "I know, who would have thought that blacks have footprints in other places besides the South. But some centers are struggling, thirsty for community support."

"Support in what way? Money?" She thought about her sons' Jamieson cousins who would whip out their checkbooks in a minute for any African American cause.

"Money is good, but like any other non-profit organizations, volunteers, donations of priceless family collections, and basically word of mouth about the museum to keep it thriving. I would like to show you the progress my sculptor and I have made so far. I'm shooting for a grand opening in time for Juneteenth."

Sandra agreed that was a good date. "Just think, blacks remained enslaved two and a half years after President Lincoln signed the Emancipation Proclamation, because they didn't get the memo per se."

"I see you know your history."

That seemed to please him. "Well, it is the oldest known national celebration commemorating the ending of American slavery. I wish that included world slavery too."

When Raimond winked, her heart fluttered. "I like the way you think. Yes, France, Portugal, Brazil, and other countries had different timelines for their *acts of humanity*." He paused and seemed to summon a different mindset, judging from his expressions. "We have local actors who are donating their time to reenact Major General Gordon Granger landing at Galveston, Texas, with U.S. Colored Troops with the word to let God's people go."

"You'll win over my sons and their cousins with your mission. They thrive on history, especially Black and African."

"I look forward to meeting them." Raimond's hand covered hers.

His stare was so intense that she needed a cool breeze to rejuvenate her. Yes, she wanted to be chased and Raimond to be her suitor. With their confessions out of the way, she was ready for the wooing to begin. Soon, they called it a night with a promise for another date the next day.

Chapter

Five

Kelsi Edwards scanned the deserted waiting room at her obstetrician's office. Rubbing her swollen belly, she shifted in her cushioned seat. Usually her husband accompanied her on doctor visits, but he was coaching a make-up game for a girls' softball team.

As athletic director for a local high school, Stephan was doing a favor for their coach who was ironically out on maternity leave.

She and Stephan had been married for five years. They tried to conceive during most of it, so when the morning sickness hit, slight weight loss and tiredness, the doctor confirmed that they were going to have a baby.

They had been downright crazy with happiness, reading baby books together, watching baby care videos, and decorating the baby's room.

A beep alerted her that Stephan had sent a text: Love you. Sorry I couldn't be there for you and my son.

Kelsi smiled as she typed. I'm the only one in the office. Where are the other pregnant ladies today? :)

They went back and forth until the girls' game was about to resume. Kelsi was about to put her cell away when she noticed that her missed calls from Raimond were now up to five. She rolled her eyes. That was one man she didn't want in the picture.

She couldn't even call him Daddy. He didn't stick around long enough for that honor. Kelsi had been devastated when he left home one night and never came back. For a long time, she had asked why until finally she didn't care anymore.

But her grief was short-lived. Two years after his disappearance, Evanston "Evan" Coleman walked into her and her mother's lives with a double portion of the love they desperately needed. She even got a baby sister out of the deal, then an annoying baby brother. Raimond became a faded memory. She, Lindsay, Tyler, her mom, and new daddy were one big happy family, so why was Raimond trying to crash her fairytale?

Evidently, he had been in town for months and then weeks ago, he started calling—no, harassing her—with a plea to talk. After the first voice mail, she hadn't bothered to listen.

Hadn't he done enough damage? At thirty-three, Kelsi had grown up without him. There was no love lost. Her parents left the choice up to her whether she wanted to reconnect with her biological father, or not. She didn't.

Picking up a baby magazine, Kelsi began to flip through it to clear her mind. Her hormones were out of whack, she had gained more weight than she and her doctor wanted, and her mood swings irritated her. Adding Raimond to the mix would only cause more drama.

The door opened and a bouncing little girl preceded her mother into the room. At least she would have company as she waited for her doctor to return from a delivery. Kelsi *ahh*ed at the girl's white polka dots on a pink skirt. Pink lace hung at the hem. The coordinating pink cardigan made Kelsi wish for a girl. The child reminded Kelsi of a princess with her brown hair brushed up in a thick ball. To cap off the outfit, the girl clutched a doll that also wore matching clothing. Kelsi definitely wanted a girl as she glanced at her expecting mother's attire.

Wow. The mother also wore polka dots, smaller ones, in a flowing dress that stopped at her ankles. Instead of a cardigan, a pastel pink shawl was draped around her shoulders. Fair skin and shoulder-length brown hair, both ladies were pretty in their pink. Yes, she and Stephan would have to try for a girl, even if she had a string of boys.

"Kennedy, go pick a seat while I sign in," the mother instructed, but the girl, who was eying Kelsi, didn't budge from her side.

That was such a charming name for an adorable little girl. Kelsi smiled at the memories of her mother dressing her and Lindsay alike.

Once the mother finished her task, she nudged her daughter toward a row of chairs on the other side of Kelsi. They both exchanged smiles.

"Mommy," Kennedy whispered loudly and pointed to Kelsi.

"Don't point."

"But, Mommy…" She patted the woman's arm.

"Kennedy." The mother's command was gentle but stern. The girl pouted. Her mommy kissed her head, which made her daughter scoot closer, but she kept her eyes on Kelsi.

"Sorry," she apologized. "My little one seems to spot an expectant mother a mile away. Is this your first one?"

"Yes," Kelsi gushed. "I'm beyond excited."

The woman giggled before introducing herself. "I'm Eva Jamieson and this sweetie pie is Kennedy."

"I'm Kelsi. You and your daughter are making me rethink this boy I'm having. I hope I can find cute outfits."

"Oh, they're out there. You just have to know where to look. My mother-in-law is a fashion personal shopper, so if she sees something she thinks Kennedy or I must have, she gets it and she won't let us reimburse her. How far along are you?"

"Six months." Kelsi grinned. "I'll have a June baby."

When Eva rubbed her stomach, Kennedy bent down and kissed her rump. The scene was so touching. "I'm fourteen weeks, so I'll have to carry this baby all summer."

"Are you having a boy or girl this time?"

Eva shrugged. "I want to be surprised."

"Not me." Kelsi shook her head. "I wanted to know."

Kennedy slipped out the chair next to Eva and raced to the kiddie corner where toys were stored in square cubes. Kelsi and Eva paused to watch her.

"I was the same way the first time. I would love to have a boy and girl, but my husband says if I give him two daughters, he's finished."

Kelsi smiled. "Two 'Daddy's little girls.' My sister and I gave my father double trouble, but he still wanted a son."

"Uh-uh, not my husband. I think Kevin—everyone calls him Kidd—would rather have double trouble than to have a boy to carry on his last name." Eva bobbed her head when Kelsi frowned. Eva nodded. "I know it doesn't make sense, but my husband still struggles with abandonment issues, since he didn't have a father in his life growing up and it's his petty way of payback not to continue the legacy, or so he thinks. I know it sounds silly that he hasn't gotten over that childhood disappointment, but God is helping him."

Kelsi's heart fluttered. "No, I understand exactly—" The nurse opened the door that separated the waiting lounge from the examining rooms.

"Mrs. Edwards."

Now? Talk about imperfect timing just when she and Eva were bonding. Kelsi sulked as she stood and followed the nurse for her weigh in. She wanted to hear more. If Eva's husband was still having desertion issues, then there was no way she was going to let Raimond back in her life to dig up bad memories. Without knowing it, Eva had given her a dose of advice as if they exchanged baby tips.

"Have a healthy and blessed pregnancy," Eva said.

"I will. You too," Kelsi was able to say before the nurse closed the door.

Chapter

Six

Sandra's lips curled into a smile, interrupting her from applying her makeup. Raimond was the culprit behind her inattentiveness. After their first dinner date, Raimond insisted they return to the scene of the "crime"—the café where they had met.

To someone looking from the outside, it would be a cheap date, but to Sandra, his gesture was sentimental as they were able to snag the same table that she had shared with Kidd.

The café had been nearly empty, but their conversations had been whispers. The experience had been surreal. Although he had to get to the museum, he didn't rush her through her meal or interrupt her as she chatted about trivial things in her life.

She sighed, staring in the mirror. Today would mark another dating adventure, so she'd better hurry and finish getting dressed. Tilting her head, Sandra scrutinized her reflection and praised God for her good health. Facial wrinkles were at a minimum, there were few gray strands, but she had a well-toned body, thanks to her exercise regimen.

In contrast, Raimond's wrinkles were limited to the laughing lines at the corners of his mesmerizing eyes; the salt-and-pepper color at his temples only accented his looks. And he wasn't slacking in the body department either. The man had some serious biceps. But the physical level wasn't the only attraction. His best feature was his full lips and the goatee that outlined them, then there was his baritone voice—wow. Raimond was intelligent and possessed an honest heart. His directness piqued her curiosity. He wouldn't play games with her. From his first bold compliment to his admission that he was to blame for the accident and his past actions, it was hard for her not to fall for him.

Sandra was blissful. They were about to begin their fourth day of a dating marathon, so Raimond was fast becoming her favorite pastime. Yet in the back of her mind, she thought about Samuel and how hard she fell for him, and kept falling until she lost in the end and two little boys were the casualties.

She thought about her hesitation at last night's dinner when he had asked to see her appointment schedule.

"Excuse me?" She froze, wondering if Raimond was about to turn into a stalker, always wanting to know her whereabouts.

"Trust me," he teased as he reached for her smartphone.

Sandra had debated how much she was willing to trust him. Even her sons didn't know her every move. Raimond waited patiently as she tried to make the best judgment call. Although he hadn't made a second request, his warm eyes seemed to say, "Trust me." Sandra had swallowed and took her chances as she placed her smartphone in his extended hand.

He tapped something into her day planner, apparently not scrolling through her appointments. When Raimond handed it back to her, Sandra had exploded with laughter. She momentarily felt ashamed for not trusting him as she read his notation: *Important new client needs your expertise with his wardrobe. Money is no object.* And he had blocked off three hours she had free anyway.

Sandra scanned his attire, blushing while Raimond seemed to be amused by her bold assessment.

The man was always meticulously dressed, so there was no need for her input. As a matter of fact, he created such a fashion statement every time she saw him that she had to double check her appearance. "You don't need my services."

"What if I need you?"

"You need me?" Sucking in her breath, Sandra got lost in the intensity of his serious expression. "You don't know me."

He looked away before facing her again. "Maybe *need* is a strong word. I want us to spend more time together." He leaned closer. "If that means mixing business with pleasure, I'll open my wallet just to be with you."

"As long as you can add God to the mix." He nodded. "Then I would love to take you on an excursion." She had perfected the art of shopping for men, which started with her sons. *Sons.* She would have to tell Ace and Kidd about Raimond soon, because it appeared they would be an item for a while.

She took a deep breath and returned to the present. Sandra had told Raimond the truth. There was enough temptation in the world and if Christ wasn't their barrier, they would fall.

I can keep you from falling, God whispered. Jude 1:24.

Sandra sighed with relief that God was in tune with her. Brushing on her mascara, she thought about Raimond and their shopping trip. She had impressed him with her talents. Her clients always told her she was the best fashion shopper that they'd used, but coming from Raimond, she felt special.

When her phone rang, she recognized Raimond's number and answered with a smile. Closing her eyes, Sandra shivered, as always, at the sound of his voice over the phone.

"Can I steal you this weekend?" His tone held mischief. "I want to show you the progress of the museum, remember?"

She turned down her lips like her granddaughter, Lauren, when she pouted. "I would love to be stolen, but I have a standing date with my granddaughters. They spend the night on most Fridays and we have a pajama party—although they're knocked out less than an hour after their baths—" she shook her head, always in awe of their unique personalities. "As their Nani, I'm never in a rush for them to leave on Saturday." But she never had a handsome gentleman vying for her time either. "We get to do girly stuff that I couldn't do with my boys."

"I'm jealous." He exhaled, not hiding his frustration. "I messed up as a father, but I'm praying that God would touch my daughter's heart and give me a chance to be a grandpa." He was silent.

Lord, please mend the broken hearts in Jesus' name. Amen, she silently prayed, then whispered, "Every girl needs her daddy. Keep reaching out to her, but give her time. She's dealing with a lot being pregnant. I'm sure she can only handle so much."

"Yeah." He sounded disappointed. "I guess you're right."

He cleared his throat and seemed to bounce back. "Let's talk about us."

Closing her eyes, Sandra allowed Raimond's words to echo within her mind. She opened them and grinned. "I would like that too. My daughters-in-law can't wait to meet you." Neither had whispered a word to their husbands yet.

Sandra made a choice of not dating while Ace and Kidd were growing up. That was then. Fast forward to the present, and both her sons had found the love of their lives and had their own families. Sandra had cut the cords, so surely, they would be happy for her. Talise and Eva convinced her not to hold off mentioning Raimond to their husbands while she got to know him better. Those two matchmakers had been as giddy as her with excitement about capturing Raimond's affection, but were mum when it came to telling their husbands.

"I'm going to an annual 70th birthday party. I'd love for you to be my guest. That way you can meet my sons and their extended families." The party was Eva and Talise's suggestion to introduce Raimond to everyone.

"I wouldn't miss it, but annual?"

"Yeah. I doubt Grandma BB will ever confess her real age." Sandra snickered. "Oh, yeah. Make sure you wear your best Stacy Adams shoes."

He chuckled. "Okay. Why?"

"Trust me. You'll find out." *And my sons will find out about you too. Lord, I'm trusting You to touch Kidd and Ace's hearts that they will like Raimond.*

Chapter
Seven

Midmorning on Friday, Raimond leaned against one of the pillars on the wrap-around porch of his six thousand foot mansion—actually it was the future home of The Heritage House Museum. The grandiose of the house reminded him of the Minnesota African American Museum and Cultural Center.

Folding his arms, he enjoyed the scenery around him while waiting for Sandra to arrive for her tour. The Central West End location was in the midst of neighborhood restoration and new construction. It was minutes away from the arts and entertainment hub of Midtown, featuring the St. Louis Symphony, the Fabulous Fox Theatre, Sheldon Concert Hall, and more. The spot was perfect.

A new black museum would be an extension of St. Louis' already documented rich African American history, besides the Dred Scott case. From entertainers, such as Josephine Baker, Kathryn Dunham, Chuck Berry, and Nelly to philanthropists Mary Meachum and her Freedom Crossing, Annie Malone, the first African American millionaire, and the segregated cemeteries that were reminders of the past.

Raimond had also visited the oldest operating black church in Missouri, First Baptist Church of St. Louis not far from downtown. But these sites were spread out and Raimond wanted to gather their history under a mini-Smithsonian in the Midwest. Everything seemed to be falling in place: the funding, artifact donations, and volunteers. Even Sandra's presence was a sunshine of blessings that God had put in his path. Yet, whenever he thought about his daughter, his vision dimmed. Kelsi's forgiveness could open the door for them to rebuild a relationship. Until that happened, Sandra was the life support that he craved.

And his craving materialized as Sandra parked her blue Nissan crossover at the curb. Grinning, Raimond jogged down the first set of steps to a wide cobblestone landing, then tackled the same number of brick steps to the sidewalk.

Sandra got out of the vehicle and walked around. Shielding her eyes from the sun with her hand, she gazed at the four-story structure before even acknowledging him.

But that didn't stop him from admiring her. He had yet to see a color or outfit that didn't complement her brown complexion or figure. Today, the two- piece suit shouted business with a sassy attitude to accomplish her goals. Her sling back heels showcased her legs. Performer Tina Turner shouldn't be the only one to have her legs insured. At least that had been the rumor.

They exhaled, "wow" at the same time for different reasons, and he reached for her hand and tugged her closer as she continued to stare at the building.

Raimond didn't rush her. The majestic entrance had the same effect on him the first time the realtor showed it to him. The owner's granddaughter was selling it for cheap to move her loved one into a nursing home.

The house still needed a lot of attention, including a new roof, but being a non-profit had its benefits when it came to community involvement. Some days Raimond had more than enough help to assist with repairs; other days, it was just him and Dace Robnett. Dace was supervising local college students' construction stages that would be used for sculpture displays.

Wait until Sandra and others saw the finished product. "Hey," Raimond said with a chuckle to break the trance the building had over her.

She blinked and faced him with eyes shining bright with awe. "This is magnificent."

He scanned her attire. "*You're* magnificent. Come on, I want to show you the progress we've made. With so much square space, the plan is to have The Heritage House serve as an intimate backdrop for meetings and private soirees to bring in revenue. It has to be multi-purpose to survive."

Taking her hand, Raimond tucked it under his arm and escorted her up the first flight of stairs. "Until it's ready for the general public, I've secured a couple of contracts with grade schools in the area to bring the museum to them."

When Sandra frowned, Raimond answered her question before she asked.

"Technology is the driving force behind any business—*any*. Because of school budget cuts, museums can no longer wait for teachers to bring students to them on a field trip. Part of my funding was invested in the digital world. Interactive displays are a big hit with students, especially artwork or old photos with QR Codes or Aurasma."

They stopped on the first landing and Sandra glanced around. He doubted she heard a word he said. Then facing him, she smiled.

"What's an Aurasma?"

So she had been paying attention. Women had conquered the world of multitasking and Sandra proved it. Raimond liked having her as his sole captive audience. "I didn't think you were listening."

"How can I not listen to you?" she said softly, squeezing his arm as a gentle wind flirted with her curls.

He stared at her, thinking, *How could I have not fallen for this beauty?*

"So what is Aurasma?" she prompted again.

"Augmented reality. It's been around for a while. Using an iPad or iPhone, a student can scan an embedded code and the picture comes to life before their eyes. Basically, it activates a video. For instance, take a picture of Misty Copeland. One minute, students are looking at a still photo, the next thing they see is our first African American principal ballerina on her toes dancing. It's a big hit with children."

Sandra nodded and continued walking. "I see so many possibilities," she stated as he opened the full-length glass door framed by thick dark wood. "The mansion was built in 1891."

As soon as they stepped inside the foyer, pounding and banging greeted their ears. "Our work in progress," Raimond reminded her as he steered Sandra in that direction.

She sucked in her breath as Raimond knew she would. "This is…" Sandra didn't finish as she strolled closer to the partially finished replica of two thrones. The oversized majestic chairs symbolized wealth and authority. A couple of walls behind the thrones were murals of the inside of an African palace. "Who are they?"

"Queen Mother of Ejisu and her brother Nana Akwasi Afrane Okpese," Dace stated as he strolled into the room, startling Sandra.

Raimond kept her close as he explained, "She's one of many female African rulers who fought against British and Portuguese colonialism."

"Exactly." Dace rocked back on his heels and stuffed his hands in his pockets. "That was one sister I would surrender to without being told twice—a beauty and bad too."

"A soul sister," Sandra said without taking her eyes off the exhibit.

"Sandra—" Raimond touched her elbow, "—this is Dace Robnett, one of the top African American sculptors in the country. He's commissioned to create The Heritage House's main exhibit *The Journey*. And he's costing me a pretty penny to do it."

"And I'm worth every half-cent." He extended his hand. "It's nice to meet you."

Once the quick introduction was made, Sandra turned her attention back on Dace's masterpiece.

Raimond eyed Dace, who was grinning as he watched Sandra's expression. The man was good—no doubt—which was why Raimond enticed him with a big chunk of his funding money to woo him to St. Louis, covering living expenses while on the project. Dace had a knack for bringing history to life with his pieces.

Museums were all about the exhibits. *The Journey* was

the exhibit that Raimond hoped would stir word of mouth publicity to keep visitors coming. Even though he planned to change exhibits to stay relevant to the community's interest, whether it was to capture current events like the protests following the shooting death of Mike Brown, or for celebrated historical events like Juneteenth.

Dace's craftsmanship preceded him. His sculptor loved history, especially African. All he needed was an audience, in which Sandra became a willing participant, and he transformed into a lecturer as they followed an imaginary Yellow Brick Road trail to another display.

"Most black museums have some type of replica of a slave ship, but I envisioned something different," Dace said peering into a glass box, It encased a 3-D display of a sunken slave ship, void of color, done in black and white. "I wanted to show our ancestors trapped," Dace said as if he was reciting inscription somewhere on the display.

But Raimond knew the words were inscribed in Dace's mind as if he had lived throughout hundreds of generations. Beside it was another glass-encased exhibit.

"It's an illusion of an aquarium," Dace continued. "Instead of beautiful fish to admire, this figure depicts slaves still in shackles in their grave in the bottom of the sea."

Sandra halted in her tracks. "This is horrible," she said, her voice shaking. Raimond wrapped his arm around her shoulders and nudged her to lean on him.

"I call this piece *The War on Freedom*," Dace explained.

"And we lost," Sandra whispered.

"No, we're still fighting. We lost some scrimmages, but the battle is the Lord's. Keep walking," Raimond whispered, then grinned, knowing what followed.

Dace had outdone himself with the six-foot sculpture of the building of the White House. It was a pristine white. The builders were dark-skinned, no doubt enslaved people.

Suddenly, Sandra activated a motion sensor that triggered a hologram of a smiling, arms folded President Barak Obama, the country's first African American president. She blinked.

"This exhibit is *The Journey.*" Dace grinned and puffed out his chest. "I wanted to remind people that black folks' history didn't begin in America as enslaved people, but in African royalty."

"Mission accomplished," Sandra mumbled as Raimond tugged her out the room, but not before she turned around and glanced at the African queen and ruler again.

"There are two more exhibits I want to show you." When she gave Raimond a pensive look, he added, "Nothing depressing."

"I don't know how that's possible with the recorded history of white racism in this country." She sighed.

He nodded. "Yes, but we can't let the evil overshadow God's goodness. There were some courageous white people who fought alongside us. Some were Freedom riders, and others assisted in the escape of thousands of enslaved people through the Underground Railroad route. Since time began, I've learned reading my Bible, that in this world, it's a spiritual warfare that we have to fight... '*For we wrestle not against flesh and blood, but against principalities, against powers, against the rulers of the darkness of this world, against spiritual wickedness in high places.*'"

She smiled. "I know that's in Ephesians 6." She stared into his eyes. "You're one endearing man. Thank you for coming into my life."

"The feeling is mutual." Easily distracted by her smile, Raimond had to fight the urge to kiss her, a moment he eagerly awaited. He glanced away before being drawn back to her. "It's important that as we tell our stories, we add a spiritual solution, not to repay evil for evil. That's Romans 12:17. It's a Scripture I constantly recall when I read, see, or hear about horrific crimes against blacks. I don't want to see anyone mistreated and I don't care what color they are. God created us all."

Resting her hand on his forearm again, she continued walking. "Thanks for creating *The Journey* that shows our lives began before the American shore and ending with the first black president."

They walked down the hall where a replica Arch, similar to the St. Louis Gateway Arch graced the entrance of a large room that was still in disarray.

"I haven't figured out the floor plan yet, I have a colleague back in D.C., who is vetting some sketches I might like. Townsend Shaw isn't a Dace Robnett, but he knows how to use space when it comes to a collection. Since the institute is in Washington, he put together an impressive exhibit on the achievements of African American women in the United States military, such as Cathay Williams who enlisted in the army just so she could serve as a Buffalo soldier in 1866. He also included present day high-ranking African American women such as Major General Marcia M. Anderson. In here—"

He walked farther into the room and his voice echoed. "I would like to highlight local African Americans who made contributions to the world like Tina Turner, Josephine Baker, Scott Joplin, Dred Scott, Katherine Durham, Grace Bumbry,

Slave Celia, Dianne White, Annie Malone, John Meachum—"

Sandra touched his arm. "I get it," she said softly.

Raimond could only stare at her lips. "Sorry. I do get carried away, but this is our history, black and white."

"This is so impressive." She spun around. "I'm proud of you, but I guess coming from the Smithsonian, I shouldn't be surprised."

Raimond couldn't tame his nostrils from flaring. "Thanks for reminding me why you're so beautiful—inside and out—and why I'm blessed to be with you." He watched as his compliments made her blush like a teenager. He liked that.

"I do have one complaint. What about blacks' contribution to the fashion world—like my hero June Horne, trailblazer at Saks as a senior buyer or Helen Williams, the first African American model in the 1950s that was rejected in this country, but went on to grace the runways in France. Or Ann Lowe, an African American, who designed Jacqueline Kennedy's wedding dress." She took a breather as she seemed to gather steam. "Of course, before that was Elizabeth Keckley, born enslaved, but purchased her freedom to become Mary Todd Lincoln's dress designer and speaking of African American designers, what about Zelda Wynn Valdes—also the black designer of the Playboy Bunnies costumes, black celebrities—"

Laughing, Raimond held up both hands in surrender. "How much more funding do I need to put you on the payroll? You're..." he leaned closer, "...incredible."

She shrugged and *hmph*ed. "I would work for free." Her eyes lit up as she followed the winding staircase to a second floor landing, then turned around to face him with a giddy expression. "A mock designer's studio on the landing and with a couple of dress forms—I could create some period costumes and other props..."

Refreshing. Finally, Raimond had met his match. Of all the women in his past, none of them could appreciate preservation of African American history and artifacts, even if it was fashion. He sighed in contentment. "Yes, to anything you say."

She laughed. "Good, I guess you're buying me a late lunch."

"I guess I am." He slipped his arm around her waist and backtracked to the entrance, waving at some students and Dace.

At the door, she stopped and placed a fist on her hip and tilted her head. She was staring at him.

"What's wrong?"

Sandra twisted her lips. "Something has been bugging me since I arrived." Reaching up, she tugged on his tie until it loosened.

Raimond's heart raced. Sandra was a temptress. Under the hood of his lashes, he watched her as she gnawed on her perfectly pouty lips, concentrating on retying his tie. She was quick and when she seemingly was satisfied with her handiwork, she stepped back and pulled him to a mirror. "See?"

Raimond blinked at the artistry. "A woman of many talents."

"It's called a peek-a-boo knot." She grinned.

"And this is called a kiss." Raimond brushed his lips against hers, waiting for permission.

When her lids fluttered closed, Raimond took that as a *yes.* He hadn't kissed a woman in years, so that had to be the reason he began to pant, but he didn't want to stop, so he placed soft pecks on her willing lips.

Hmmm. Raimond could put on another tie again without thinking of her gentle manipulation, determined expression, and her sweet smelling perfume. And those full lips that begged for a kiss and he delivered it with constraint in mind. They both were practicing Christians and Jesus would keep them from falling, if they wanted to be kept. "Yeah," he mumbled to himself. He had already fallen into a life of sin and he didn't want to repeat it.

Raimond pulled back. They were in sync opening their eyes. Sandra appeared to be in a daze as she leaned forward and rested her head on his chest.

No words were spoken as Raimond got his breathing under control. "Does this mean we're exclusive?"

She glanced up and smiled. "Yes."

Then he kissed her again.

Chapter

Eight

"I'm in a happy place right now, Raimond. I have a good husband and a loving father," Kelsi stated when she answered his call before he could say, hello. "Leave me alone," she snapped, then his only daughter disconnected without a goodbye.

Bowing his head in defeat, Raimond stared at his phone. *That was not a good way to begin his Saturday*, he thought, as Kelsi's stinging rebuke lingered. He needed a few minutes to recover. Yes, he was reaping what he sowed, but he hadn't counted on repenting for his sins and making amends. Otherwise, he would have considered his choices more carefully.

Your sin is too great to forgive, the devil taunted him.

I have forgiven you. Trust in Me, God superseded the declaration.

"Trust," Raimond repeated. He had trusted God when he moved from D.C., he trusted Jesus when he searched for a place for the museum, and he even trusted that God knew what He was doing when he approached Sandra. But trusting Him for Kelsi's compassion was proving to be more challenging.

Raimond wasn't one to dwell in a pity party state, so he stood, slipped on his athletic shoes, and swiped his keys off one of his few remaining unopened boxes. One of the selling perks of the apartment was a workout center and that's where he was going to clear his head. He texted Townsend as he rode the elevator to the lobby.

I don't know how much rejection a father can take. Kelsi basically says she has no room for me.

In the gym, he nodded at another resident and programmed his favorite treadmill. He had logged five minutes on his cardio workout by the time Townsend called.

"Awww, man, I'm sorry you have to go through this. I wish she could see how great a guy you are." His friend sounded as frustrated as he felt.

"Thanks, but I don't blame my daughter's hatred toward me." He heard it in her voice and sensed it in his spirit. "I had a chance with her and I blew it." Raimond adjusted the incline on the treadmill.

"So now what?"

Nothing is impossible for Me, God whispered. *I speak and it is accomplished.*

Then speak, Lord, make this easy for me, Raimond wanted to demand, but Jesus held the power, so Raimond had no choice but to stay in his place. "I'm sure God is working behind the scenes." He had to believe it. Yes, he was convinced that God could move the barricades. "Jesus saved me when I didn't know I needed Him. The Lord can open the door to my daughter's heart, so I can walk through and plead my case."

Townsend grunted. "Are you sure you don't want me to be your character witness and talk to her? You said we're about the same age."

"No, but thanks for offering." Raimond smiled and grabbed a towel to wipe the sweat off his face. "I'm going to keep praying and trying in that order."

"Well, o-okay. If that doesn't work, I'm here," Townsend answered.

Despite his confidant being in his corner, Raimond knew his friend didn't understand his level of faith. Sometimes, Raimond was blown away by the measure of faith the Lord had given him. "Prayer works."

They ended the call without Townsend questioning another comment about the Lord. Raimond checked the number of calories he had burned at his pace. He thought about Sandra. She was in his corner too, when it came to his goal of reconciling with Kelsi, but he didn't want to burden her with each play-by-play defeat with his daughter. Most times, they ended their conversations with the Lord on their lips, either with "I pray God blesses your day," or "Take Jesus with you."

Raimond left the gym with his body rejuvenated, but his spirit still down. Back in his apartment, he reached for his Bible. "Lord, I thank You for the blessings You have given me in my life, but I need an encouraging word from You about Kelsi please. In Jesus' name. Amen." Opening his bedroom door, Raimond stepped on the balcony that overlooked Forest Park on one side and the Arch as a backdrop in the other direction. He flipped through the pages until his spirit urged him to stop at 1 Corinthians 13:7: *Love bears all things, believes all things, hopes all things, and endures all things.* He continued reading until the last verse of the chapter, but verse seven seemed to ripple through his mind. "Amen, Lord."

As if he had just digested an energy drink, Raimond stood and went back inside to shave, then shower for the birthday party he was accompanying Sandra to in a few hours. This was a big deal in their relationship. He had never been to her condo. For almost a week, they had met for breakfast, lunch, or dinner. Next, he would meet her circle of friends and family. Things were falling in place for them as a couple. All he needed was for Kelsi to be a part of his life.

When it was time for him to dress, he scanned his shoe collection in his closet. Sandra had requested that he wear his best Stacy Adams shoes, but she didn't mention whether it was a suit and tie affair. Shaking his head at his clothes, Raimond wished he was wearing a suit, so Sandra could play with his tie.

After dressing casually, Raimond was out the door and en route to Sandra's gated community. He refused to allow his morning conversation with Kelsi ruin the rest of his day with Sandra. "God, you said to give you my burdens.

I'm still waiting, God whispered. *Reread 1 Peter 5:7.*

Raimond was frustrated as he pushed the knob on his satellite radio and soft instrumental gospel music filled his SUV. "He was trying his best to let go of that stress." By the time he knocked on her door a half-hour later, peace was rooted within him. When Sandra opened the door, his joy was complete. The woman in red was stunning, even if it was a simple flowing dress.

"You're gorgeous!"

"Thank you, come in." She stepped back and when he stepped in, Raimond heard the paw taps of Boston, her Yorkie. When Sandra told him that her pet had been her constant companion, Raimond knew he had to switch places with the pooch.

Sliding his hands in his pants pockets, Raimond admired her place. The living room had the right mixture of colors and flair for a showplace, but homey. Sandra should add interior decorator to her résumé. Her skills would definitely complement an exhibit at the museum.

"I need a hug." He opened his arms and Sandra filled them. They held each other tightly, quietly, letting their heartbeats speak to each other. "You smell good," he whispered.

"Thank you," she murmured against his chest and he gently rested his chin on the top of her head.

As Raimond loosened his hold, Sandra looked up and concern was reflected in her eyes. "Is everything all right?"

"It is now." He smiled and brought her hands to his lips and brushed a kiss on them before gracing her lips with a kiss.

"Behave, Mr. Mayfield." She giggled, then coaxed Boston into his kennel while he watched.

The hem of her dress teased her toned ankles and his hormones. There was something to be said about a woman who had command of high heels and Sandra moved in them with ease.

"Ready." Sandra gathered a small tote bag.

Hand in hand, they strolled to his SUV. Happiness draped him. He felt foolish for being so bummed out earlier about Kelsi. He had a prayer partner who could help him weather the rejections. "Do you want me to carry your bag?"

"Oh, no. It's not heavy." Mischief danced in her eyes.

Inside his vehicle, Raimond programmed Grandma BB's address into his GPS. He drove with one hand while keeping a connection to Sandra with his other.

She chatted about her proposed fashion exhibit at his museum. Her excitement was contagious and he couldn't wait for her vision to materialize.

Raimond smirked. Sandra was carefree and drama-free, which stabilized his life right now with Kelsi's rejection.

Soon, they entered the township of Old Ferguson. "Wow." Raimond was in awe of the large houses that reminded him of the one he purchased for the museum in the city.

"I said the same thing when I saw them. Many are listed on the National Register of Historic Places." She pointed to a house that was built from material from the 1904 World's Fair, another was once owned by Barbecue gigantic Louis Maull, and another one had a wide door to conduct wakes. Raimond soaked in every tidbit as Sandra chatted away. "Grandma BB and Cheney Jamieson took me on the walking tours. When the Ferguson riots broke out, these hidden neighborhoods weren't touched. Clashes were basically near the apartment complex where Michael Brown lived and in front of the Ferguson Police station."

Before Raimond could ask Sandra her thoughts about the police shooting, his mouth dropped open at the number of cars lining the side streets to their destination on Benton.

"Do you think all these people are at the party?"

"Oh, yes. She throws some interesting parties."

Curious, Raimond gave her a side glance. "How interesting?"

"You'll see." She turned her head, hiding whatever telltale expression she wore.

Parking blocks away, Raimond assisted Sandra out as she refused curb service at the door. He was concerned about her walking in those heels as Raimond intertwined his fingers with her dainty ones. They enjoyed the unhurried stroll on the winding sidewalks canopied with old trees along the way.

"Thank you for coming into my life," Raimond said for the umpteenth time, bringing her hand to his lips.

Sandra leaned into him. "I think you bombarded my life, but I have no regrets."

"Good. Me neither." He chuckled. Being with Sandra felt right and he was falling for her and fast.

They admired the homes, commenting on the architecture, landscaping, and the feel of the neighborhood until they turned the corner. The party house was easily identifiable by the loud music and a steady stream of guests entering...and two squad cars?

Squeezing Sandra's hands, Raimond tugged her closer. "Should we be concerned that the police were called?"

"They're probably on the guest list." She shrugged.

As guests or on security detail because of perceived chaos? Raimond wondered, but didn't ask. The woman's story-and-a-half house was striking with three dormers overlooking an immaculate lawn. As they approached the doorway, people spilled out before they could knock. A shirtless bear of a dark-skinned man greeted them, or rather his companion. Raimond didn't like the appreciative glance he gave his date.

"Hi, San." He wiggled his eyebrows mischievously.

"Hi, Stan."

He blushed then frowned when he eyed Raimond. "Who's your friend?" He scanned Raimond's attire, focusing on his feet. He twisted his lips.

"This is my guest, Raimond Mayfield."

"Ah, okay." Stan nodded. "You better slip those bad boys on before Grandma BB sees you."

Sandra pulled a pair of men's shoes—Stacy Adams—out of the tote bag hanging on her shoulder, leaving Raimond lost for words. She dropped them on the floor, stepped out of her strappy heels, then wiggled her black nail-polished toes as she slipped her feet into the shoes. They were a stylish red with red stitching that complemented her dress—wait a minute. She was wearing men's shoes to a party?

"Ready." She beamed as she stuffed her shoes into the bag.

Inside, Raimond stared at the guest makeup. He could tell the ethnic background from the garbs: African, Indians, Asians, and other outerwear that he couldn't pinpoint the origin. Yet, they were in sync on the dance floor. "First question—" he was about to ask when Sandra must have read his mind.

"In honor of Grandma BB's annual 70th birthday party, guests wear Stacy Adams shoes," she shouted over the music.

Raimond didn't know which part to question, the shoes or the annual part. "How many times has she turned seventy?"

Sandra shrugged. "Take a guess. Here she comes now."

"San," the petite woman said with a wave of a hand, then exchanged air kisses with Sandra.

The party girl's silver hair was piled on top of her head in a ball and large hooped earrings tugged at her earlobes. The fashion statement looked too painful in his opinion, especially for a senior citizen. If she was going for the sexy look with her off-the-shoulder top loaded down with rhinestones, she lost him.

Neither one of his deceased grandmothers would have dared worn them, nor would they have been caught in his grandfathers' shoes either, such as the spectator white-and-black Stacy Adams Grandma BB boasted on her feet.

As if sensing his observation, the host faced him and squinted—could that be a sign of aging? "So this is your *young* man, Raimond, you say?"

"Yes." It was good to know that he was talked about. Puffing out his chest, he extended his hand. Instead of shaking it, Grandma BB squatted and examined his shoes as if she was the sales person. "Hmm-mm. Those are from the 2012 spring collection. Good taste and I bet you got them at a good price—on clearance."

Speechless, Raimond didn't know how to respond as the woman stood, craned her neck, and held his stare. "Raimond Mayfield." She scrunched her nose, twisted her mouth, then rolled her eyes as if she was working every muscle in her face. "I'll have a nickname for you before you leave."

"That's what she does." Sandra squeezed his bicep and whispered, "It's an initiation of sorts...I'm San," she explained.

"Okay." He smiled and winked at Sandra before facing Grandma BB again. "Then I look forward to it."

Grandma BB twisted her lips again. "Don't be, but that's a good answer." She spun around about to walk away when more Stacy Adams-wearing women joined them.

They gave him appreciative smiles and Sandra unwrapped her arm from his and linked their hands. Her face glowed as she made the introductions. "Raimond, these are my beautiful daughters-in-law, Eva Jamieson, married to my oldest son, Kidd, and Talise, married to Ace."

"Nice to meet you." Raimond nodded and when he extended his hand, they both accepted.

"We've heard a lot about you," the woman introduced as Talise said.

"It's nice to finally put a face to this incredible voice Sandra raves about," Eva added.

Lifting an eyebrow, he glanced at Sandra and lowered his voice. "Really?" When she blushed, Raimond easily forgot about their audience. His heart pounded as their attraction intensified.

"I'm withholding my sentiments until I get a thorough background check on you," Grandma BB said with a straight face, shattering their private moment. "I have a fingerprint kit."

She whistled to summon one of the officers. He seemed annoyed to leave the dance line.

Adjusting his belt around his waist Officer Walsh went from "party mode" to "on duty." With a suspicious glare at Raimond, he asked, "What's going on, Grandma BB, do you suspect him of criminal activity?"

Raimond was about to protest when the officer spared him—the guest of honor shook her head and her shoulders slumped. "Not yet."

"It's her scare tactics as part of her initiation," Sandra whispered as her lips brushed his ear, accidentally or intentionally, but his nostrils flared. "Be a good sport and play along."

He was too old to play games and when it came to the

police or any other man, and he didn't take kindly to being disrespected.

The officer folded his arms and squinted at Grandma BB. "Now, what did I tell you last time? I can't violate a person's civil liberty, because of the way they smell, walk, or the color of their underwear," he scolded her with a tone of reverence.

"You missed the point. I didn't want to see that chile's underwear," Grandma BB snapped. "Fine, I'll do it myself." She twirled and wormed her way back on the dance floor.

The officer smiled and mouthed, *Sorry* to Raimond, then shrugged and joined Grandma BB. They moved to the music without missing a step.

"Whew." Raimond relaxed his shoulders. Here he was worried about his drama when Sandra had plenty to spare. "Is she okay? Did she miss taking her medicine, or something?"

"No." Talise shrugged. "She's normal."

Eva chuckled. "Plus, she doesn't take any medicine."

"Maybe she should," Raimond mumbled as Sandra had him meet more Jamiesons than he could remember, laughing and snacking along the way. Despite the rough start, he was having a fantastic time with Sandra.

Chapter Nine

The warning bells didn't go off in Kidd's head until it was too late. He almost choked on his own air at his mother's entrance on the arms of some mystery man. Who was he, what did he want with his mother?

Before he could cross the room to get answers to his question, Eva intercepted his path with their daughter in her arms.

"Dad-da," Kennedy called as she reached for him.

With an angelic face like her mother's, he gave his daughter all his attention. "How's my girl?" He smothered a kiss into her freshly shampooed and braided hair.

"Watch the baby. I see Sandra and her guest. I'm going to speak to them." Eva graced him with a smile that had a tad of mischief in it.

"I'll go with you." Kidd was about to match her step when she stopped him.

"No, no. She'll introduce you when she's ready." With

69

that, she left him standing there, watching her mingle with other dancers as she strategically made her way to the other side of the room.

"Hmm-mm." Kidd squinted. His wife knew something. When Eva relayed the message that his mother was bringing a guest to the party, Kidd didn't think twice that it was probably a client, neighbor, or one of her walking buddies he had met. But a man? His wife was an accomplice, abetting a stranger who had yet to be cleared by him. How could his wife betray him like that?

Kidd didn't like being in the dark with anything or anyone concerning his mother. He was itching to risk breaking through the Soul Train line—a no-no at Grandma BB's parties—to confront the stranger.

He should have known something was up when Grandma BB shuffled across the floor to the door, snapping her fingers, and welcomed them. She very seldom left the floor, priding herself on out-dancing all her guests. "Don't stop the music," she yelled. "Carry on." The DJ obeyed.

Now Talise had joined Eva—the two traitors—and they were chatting away with the man. Whose side were they on anyway?

Ace moseyed on up beside him, holding Lauren and bobbing his head. "Did you see—"

"Yep." Kidd hadn't let them out of his sight.

"Do you know who—"

"Nope."

Soon their older cousin, Parke, joined them and slapped a hand on Kidd's shoulder. He tensed. "You'll meet him. Be patient."

Was he that transparent? Kidd wondered.

Ace laughed. "My brother was born with impatience in his DNA. Mom said he cried before he needed a diaper change."

"Funny. In case you haven't noticed, Ma hasn't even looked our way," Kidd complained.

"Bro, there are a lot of people here."

"And your point is?" Kidd grunted. "It's not like anyone could overlook a group of black men huddled in a corner."

His mother always said it was her sons' good looks, but truth be told, Kidd, Ace, and his cousins, Parke, Malcolm, and Cameron were all close to the same build, weight, and height. And when they were together, they could present a united force to be reckoned with.

Parke folded his empty arms. His children were older. His youngest son, Chase, was somewhere around here wreaking havoc, because he refused to be confined. The four-year-old was definitely living up to his name.

"At ease, cuz," Parke said. "Grandma BB is scoping him out, I'm sure. She can see right through a person and one thing my daughter has picked up from Grandma BB's, 'she's going to tell it like it is.' She's probably already guessed his shoe size. I'm sure before the night is over, she'll have his credit report and background check results in her inbox. She's just that good."

"Humph." Yes, Grandma BB was good at snooping and causing drama whenever she crushed the soles of her Stacy Adams, but that didn't appease Kidd. He collided with the infamous Grandma BB when he was coerced to work undercover as the resident liaison at the nursing facility where she was convalescing after suffering a stroke. The best thing that came out of that covert assignment meeting his wife, the former Eva Savoy, and he wouldn't let her get away.

All that happened at a time in Kidd's life when he resented being a Jamieson and had resisted his cousins' goodwill gestures as a handout. But the tables turned when the family got the word that Grandma BB had been rushed to the hospital with the silent killer.

Once the facts were ironed out, Kidd learned that Grandma BB owned a retired police dog she had named Silent Killer, whose vocal cords had been injured in the line of duty. And she had suffered a stroke and was very much alive but in need of rehab.

Parke and the others tapped Kidd for the job when Grandma BB refused visitors, bearing the last name Jamieson, because she didn't want anyone seeing her in that condition. It was a good thing since she had yet to meet Kidd. Even with a partial stroke, her antics triggered the facility to request the SWAT to locate her whereabouts when she went missing on the common ground.

Grandma BB might be a tough cookie, but Kidd was his mother's sole protector and he took that seriously. He had waited long enough. The only thing that stood in the way was the sleeping daughter in his arms. Just then, Parke's only daughter and family's babysitter-in training, Kami, came to his rescue.

"Can I hold her, Uncle Cousin?"

Once an odd endearment, Kidd stopped long ago trying to correct Parke's children when it came to addressing him. They were like eighth or ninth cousins—he always forgot. Since he was close to their father's age, they insisted on calling him uncle.

He watched as Kami, now eleven years old, cuddled his daughter in her arms and glowed with joy. She loved to play with dolls and babies and the Jamiesons kept the girl busy.

Straightening his body, he flexed his biceps and started toward his targets. With the dance floor separating them, Kidd swayed from side to side as he dared not cause someone to misstep as the song ended. He was almost there when Eva came into his view with an innocent smile that he didn't trust. "Hi, babe, doesn't your mother look stunning?"

"Yeah. She looks all right..." Suddenly, the DJ played the popular Wobble song and more guests stormed to the dance floor. Kidd swept his wife in his arms and got her out of the maze so she wouldn't get bumped, stepped on, or swung at.

He ushered them into a private nook and sat her on his lap. She wrapped her arms around his neck and puckered her lips for a kiss.

Gritting his teeth, Kidd played her game, but he refused to submit to her charms when he wanted answers. "So this is your doing?"

Tilting her head, Eva smirked. "No, honey. I guess you can take the credit," she said smugly.

"Me?" He frowned.

"Yes. They met the day you took Sandra out to breakfast. It was so sweet how he got her attention."

"He hit a car in the process," Talise chimed out of nowhere as she and Ace took the seat across from them, sipping on *unspiked lemonade for the saints* as Grandma BB always labeled the pitcher.

"What!" Kidd roared and waited for Ace's reaction.

Figured his brother said nothing, draping an arm around his wife and scooting her closer. Ace always was laid back, unfazed, and easygoing unless he felt his wife and child were threatened.

Kidd huffed. Some things he would have to do on his own, and his priority was shielding his mother from another heartache from a man like his father. He stirred to get up, but his wife shifted her baby weight on his legs.

She cupped his face in her hands. "Kevin Jamieson, Sandra is a big girl and she's glowing. Let her be happy."

"I know nothing about this dude. What's his name? What does he do for a living?" He squinted at his wife who simply rubbed her stomach.

"The baby and I are hungry, so do you mind helping me fix a plate?"

Of course, he did, and she knew it. But he denied her nothing, so he did as she had asked. As soon as the gifts were opened and the party wound down, Kidd would get a full account of this man's intentions. Until then, Kidd would keep one eye on him.

Grandma BB's parties were like all night dance-a-thons. It was getting late and Kidd was ready to get his family home. But his mother had yet to bring her mystery man anywhere close to him. The man kept his arm around his mother's private parts—the waist, which was inches away from her behind. Close enough for him to defend her honor.

While Eva was saying her goodbyes, Kidd made his way to the couple. "Ma." He kissed her cheek, then looked at her date. "And you are?"

"I'm Raimond—with an 'i' Mayfield." He extended his hand with a smile that looked crooked to him. "And you're Kevin, the one everybody calls Kidd."

"Don't let the nickname fool you."

As the man talked, Kidd didn't break eye contact. The deeper he searched for some underlining deceit, all he envisioned was Samuel Jamieson about to destroy the life of a young naïve woman with a promising career.

Red flags flashed before Kidd. He gripped Raimond—with an 'i'—in a shake meant to intimidate, but the man met his challenge. Kidd refused to back down and apparently, neither did his mother's suitor.

"Kevin." His mother's deceptively sweet voice hinted for him to cease and desist. "That's enough."

He got one last squeeze in before complying. When they did disengage, both exercised their fingers to regain blood circulation.

"Ma, I didn't know you were seeing anyone."

"You don't need to know all my business, son. You have your own family that needs your attention, so now you know about Raimond."

"But I don't." Folding his arms, he faced the man. "So how did you meet my mother?"

Raimond and his mother exchanged a silly expression and chuckled. "I walked up to Sandra and told her how beautiful she is."

Mom, you fell for that line? "Do you always hit on women—figuratively or literally?" Kidd made sure his tone had an edge to it.

"Son." His mother upped him with a warning tone of her own, then capped it off with a smile.

"I don't, but I couldn't resist. When I walked away, I realized that there was something special about her and I wanted a chance to know what." The man cast a goofy glance at his mother, which caused her to giggle.

Kidd gritted his teeth. The man's lines were so outdated that he wouldn't be surprised that Samuel Jamieson had said the very same thing to mislead his mother. Well, not again. He would not let another man hurt her.

"Sandra literally stopped traffic."

His mother leaned into Raimond and the man was swift to put his arm around her shoulder and rubbed her arm, a gesture too intimate a scene for public display.

"No, it was your fender bender that did that." She covered her face shamefully and started laughing. "I can't believe you were honking your horn and yelling out the window in an upscale shopping area."

Somebody behind Kidd said, "Uh-oh," and they were right. How disrespectful. "I have a problem with this scenario. My mother is a woman of integrity—"

"Bro." Ace nudged him. "Let's talk in private." It wasn't a request as Ace bumped him toward the back of Grandma BB's house.

Kidd quietly went along as his cousins eyed him. "I got this." Although Parke, Malcolm, and Cameron nodded, their expressions stated otherwise.

"No you don't," his wife stated, rolling her eyes. "Talise, I think our presence is mandatory."

Once all six were behind closed doors in the sunroom, Sandra and Raimond took a seat, looking a little too chummy for Kidd as he paced the floor. Eva looked uncomfortable as if she was ready to give birth instead of being only a few weeks shy of five months pregnant.

The old grandfather clock ticked away annoyingly. Otherwise, the guests' voices were muffled on the outside the door. No one seemed to be in a hurry as they waited him out.

Finally, Kidd stopped and eyed the pair as if he was about to interrogate Kennedy's first date, which would not happen until she was twenty-one, if he had anything to say about it. "So, Raimond, it sounds like you didn't make a good first impression—"

"On the contrary." His mother reached for Raimond's hand and Kidd documented every movement, from the linking of their fingers to Raimond's thumb rubbing hers. Kidd counted to three to tame his reaction. "He got my attention and I think it was sweet."

But you don't know this man's intentions, Kidd wanted to warn her.

I see all things, God whispered. *I'm all-knowing. Reread Psalms 33:13-15.*

Kidd swallowed. Suddenly, he felt like a small boy again. *But You didn't intervene then, Lord. I have to protect her. She's my mother. I can't stand by and let her get hurt again.* After letting God know where he stood, Kidd proceeded, "So where are you from?"

Raimond answered without hesitation, "I have roots in Orleans, but my family moved to St. Louis when I was a boy. Then I moved to D.C., and now I've recently relocated back here."

"Why?"

Kidd watched as a bit of his confidence slipped and Raimond looked away. What was he hiding?

"I wanted to reestablish a relationship with my daughter." His voice cracked but his eyes never wavered from Kidd's.

Reestablish? What had Raimond done? "Have you been or are you presently married?"

"Kidd!" His mother shot him daggers.

"I was married a long time ago. I wasn't the best father or husband back then."

Something snapped inside Kidd. Suddenly, Raimond vanished and Samuel Jamieson materialized. "But you're a better man now?" He squinted.

"Yes, I am." Raimond held his stare. "I've been washed in the Blood of Jesus and redeemed by the baptism of the Holy Ghost."

Coming from anybody else that testimony would have gotten a Hallelujah from Kidd, but not today. How did he know this wasn't a church decoy sitting before him? "I see."

Kidd didn't remember what question he asked next for Raimond to say, "My past and present are an open book. I take full responsibility of my actions that caused my wife to file for divorce and for abandoning my daughter."

Another child abandonment? "You had an affair or affairs, didn't you?" Kidd challenged him. "You and the man who fathered me have something in common, problems with faithfulness. We didn't know Samuel was married until I was almost a teenager. Do you have any idea how his careless actions ruined our lives?" he roared.

"Babe, calm down." His wife came to his side and stroked his arm. It was soothing, but not enough. "He repented and his sins were forgiven."

This time, his mother stood, but she didn't make a move toward him. "Kevin Jamieson, we all have confessions. You didn't know that Samuel was married until then, but I suspected before I got pregnant with Ace. But by that time, I still loved him and I never wanted to know the truth."

"So you knew?" Kidd's eyes blurred. "You knew?" he repeated.

She nodded and cast a painful look. "Why do you think I went to church that Sunday and repented? God forgave me and I have lived holy to this present day, so don't be so hard on Raimond," she said, her voice softening. "I was—*past tense*—just as guilty."

Kidd's heart exploded after what he just heard. "You were okay with being a married man's other woman? Ma!?" He never suffered asthma as a child, but he felt like an attack was in progress.

Suddenly, the door burst open. Grandma BB appeared as if she had hands on holsters on her hips. The other Jamiesons stood behind her as if they were her backup. "What's going on in here?"

Uh-oh, that woman was crazy and Kidd had been witness to some of her antics, like discharging a weapon, but her services weren't needed. "Nothing now." Kidd couldn't comprehend the thought of his upstanding mother, ruining another family.

"If there is going to be a fight up in my house, I'm going to start and end it."

There was nothing to fight about anymore. "We're leaving anyway," Kidd said and ushered his wife out the room without any goodbye kisses, hugs, or handshakes. He scooped Kennedy out of Kami's arms and in a daze, kept walking until he reached his vehicle. He secured Kennedy in her car seat and helped a silent Eva inside and waited until she clicked her seat belt.

"I can't believe you knew," he said softly, trying to keep the hurt out of his voice. "And you never said a word to me that my own mother was dating." Without waiting for her reply, Kidd dragged his feet to the driver's side. *Lord, this hurts worse than learning the truth about my father.* His heart shed a tear that he couldn't, accepting that his mother was no longer the victim in the Samuel Jamieson fiasco, but was a willing accomplice.

Chapter

Ten

Kelsi had been on good behavior since her last doctor's appointment, watching what she ate, getting plenty of rest, and maintaining her exercise regime. But all bets were off when she and her sister were on their way to set up her baby's registry and there was a Cold Stone Creamery sighting. "Baby crave. We need to make an emergency stop for nourishment."

"Really?" Lindsay gave her a crazy look when she stopped at a light. "You do know that today's high is only supposed to get to fifty?" she griped, then shivered.

"Blame it on your nephew." Kelsi shrugged.

"The things I do for my big sister," Lindsay mumbled and when the light changed, backtracked to the shopping strip mall where the culprit was located.

Before getting out of the car, Kelsi wrapped a knit cape around her, then linked arms with her sister, who was about the same height as her five-six, and crossed the parking lot.

Inside the store, a woman behind the counter seemed too delighted to see them, considering there was only one other customer in the place.

"Can I help you, ladies?"

Kelsi didn't have to peruse the menu. "Banana Caramel Crunch," she stated then treated her sister to whatever concoction she wanted. "And you didn't have a taste for some ice cream—right," Kelsi teased, sticking out her tongue as the clerk filled their orders. Minutes later with her waffle cone in hand, Kelsi whispered her grace and did a taste test as she chose a table for them.

Fridays were designated as their sisterhood day. The end of the week worked for both of them. Lindsay was in grad school—with Fridays off—working toward her masters in physician assistant studies. When Kelsi reached three months, she had reduced her hours to part time at the Missouri Board of Education where she had met her future husband six years earlier and married one later.

Once their baby arrived, she would be a full-time mother. Stephan made good money as the athletic director at a local high school. As a matter of fact, Stephan wanted her to quit the day they got the news from the doctor.

After four years of trying to get pregnant, Kelsi and her family cried when they learned she had finally conceived. For once, Kelsi felt God had heard and answered her prayers.

Lindsay, who couldn't wait to be an aunt, volunteered for the first babysitting duty.

Growing up, the Coleman sisters were very close. When someone saw one, the other sister was usually nearby. And when Kelsi married, she felt the void, even though she was in love with Stephan. No one ever suspect they were stepsisters, because they looked so much alike. That was before Kelsi's weight gain from the pregnancy. Both inherited jet-black wavy shoulder-length hair, which they wore natural rather than use chemicals. They even had a small beauty mole beneath their left eye in almost identical places. Kelsi was a shade darker, but Lindsay matched that with summer tans.

They had similar tastes in food, clothes, and hobbies, and that's where it stopped. While Stephan's quiet strength attracted Kelsi, Lindsay preferred men who had strong personalities that clashed with hers. Go figure.

Lindsay grinned as she licked her oatmeal cookie batter. "You know I'm going all out for this baby shower." She pumped a fist in the air.

"This baby is going to be spoiled." Kelsi smiled. "Daddy's already set up a college fund and Mom is stockpiling educational toys. Of course, Stephan's parents would not be outdone. They will foot Baby Stephie's private school tuition."

Lindsay laughed, then became quiet. Something was on her mind.

"What?" Kelsi prompted.

"What about...you know, your other father?" she whispered as if the place was crowded with eavesdroppers.

Kelsi stiffened. Her sister had managed to kill the mood. "I only have one Daddy and Evanston Coleman is him," she said in a tone that conveyed the subject was over.

Seemingly accepting Kelsi's decision, Lindsay backed down and switched to themes for the baby shower. They finished their treats and left for the Babies"R"Us Superstore.

Less than ten minutes later from the time the sisters entered the store, the sisters *oohed* and *ahhed* on practically everything in the baby department. "This is so much fun and I thank God for my sister to share this experience with," Kelsi said.

"You do know that Mom and Daddy are probably going to get most of the stuff you put on the registry," Lindsay said after the clerk gave them scanning guns to begin their hunt.

Rubbing her stomach, Kelsi soothed the little one stretching in her womb, communicating that he was loved. "And I wouldn't deprive them." She beamed and pointed toward her first item. "Look at this portable changing table."

"I love the color match, blues, gray, and a touch of yellow." Lindsay became quiet and for the next couple of minutes gnawed off and on on her bottom lip. "Don't you think you're depriving your fathe—" she cleared her throat, "—I mean Raimond? Don't you have a little guilt?" Lindsay demonstrated with a small space between her thumb and finger.

Kelsi stopped scanning the cutest swing set and gave her sister a pointed look. It seemed that she couldn't bully Lindsay to silence on this one. "Evidently, Raimond had no guilt when he deserted me and our mother. I remember crying and praying for my daddy to come home. The few times he called, he and our mother argued and he hung up without talking to me. Not only was Raimond Mayfield not a decent human being, but he was a horrible parent. The father I prayed for was our daddy." Others walked by just as bubbly as she was when she first arrived, so Kelsi lowered her voice. "Please, sis, after almost thirty years this is a cold case. When Daddy adopted me, I erased all memories of Raimond. Now, I wish he'd go back to wherever he came and stop harassing me. I have more important things to worry about than him.

This pregnancy has already been stressful with the weight gain, migraines… Stephan is waiting for me to give him the word and he will rough Raimond up."

Lindsay cringed. "I still think the little girl in you needs closure, otherwise, you would've given Stephan the go-ahead the first time Raimond called."

Why did Lindsay even care? "You're supposed to be on my side." But her sister did have a point, which was why Stephan had no idea how many times Raimond had left voice messages.

"All I'm saying is if you do want to meet with him, you know we'll all support your decision, even Daddy."

"Hmm-mm." Kelsi strolled ahead. Her sister didn't know that she had already had this conversation with their parents. *"I didn't want you to be caught off guard," Ivy had said while Kelsi was visiting.*

Kelsi had to remember to take a deep breath. "Well, I am," she had snapped, then apologized. "I wish you had asked my permission first before giving a stranger my number."

"And you would have said 'no' and that would have been based on childhood memories. In hindsight, I wish I had spoken to you if I'd known he would have hounded you."

Evidently, her mother's memories must have dulled. "Daddy, are you sure you are okay with me talking to Raimond?" Kelsi was fearful that it would crush her father's feelings that she had given away his rightful place in her life.

"He doesn't threaten my love for you, princess." Evan winked. "You will always be Daddy's girl who can come to me for hugs, love, comfort, money." They laughed.

Her mother's smile had been genuine. "When your father

left, I was angry and bitter. He was a poor excuse for a husband and a sad case for a father, but it was your grandmother who drilled into me that you were the one who would suffer the most if I used you against him." Ivy took a deep breath, then continued, "It was a struggle and it took me a while, but I made up my mind that I would never stop him from seeing you and when I met this man here," she said as she squeezed Evan's knee, "he agreed to love you with no boundaries, even though the door would always be left open for Raimond. We never heard from him until now."

"His timing couldn't be worse." Kelsi gritted her teeth.

"I thought about that too," her mother had said.

Her father rested his arm around her mother's shoulder and snickered. "In your mother's defense, I did turn the other ear when she chewed him out royally. I felt she had every right for what he put her through and he deserved her wrath."

Ivy Coleman gave her a repentant look. "Believe me, he called for months. The last time, your father got on the phone and backed me up that if he was serious, he basically better make you a priority, even if that meant moving back here."

"We called his buff, princess," her father added and gave her a hug. "And he answered. My parents never abandoned me and of course, every family has secrets, but we have reared you to be a beautiful young woman and it's up to you to decide the type of relationship you want with Raimond. Whatever your choice, make sure it's what you want and we will back you. Otherwise, we'll be the fly on the wall that will swim in to rescue you if you find this isn't what you want."

Kelsi pulled her mother and daddy into a group hug. "I have the best parents in the world."

Lindsay bumping her pulled Kelsi back into the present. "Did you finish your guest list?" Lindsay changed the subject to Kelsi's relief. She owed Raimond nothing, including her time.

Lindsay looped one arm through Kelsi's and steered her toward the big- ticket items.

"All one hundred people I could think of." Kelsi giggled when Lindsay's eyes widened in shock. "Just kidding. I have thirty names… But I would like to invite this one expectant mother I met in my doctor's office. I connected with her. There was something about her I liked."

"Besides being pregnant?"

Kelsi bumped her sister back. "Hmm-mm. She had this glow about her. I should have exchanged numbers to stay in contact and go shopping or something, but the nurse called me to see the doctor."

"Hey." Lindsay rubbed Kelsi's stomach as if to wake up her nephew. "Don't try to give away my spot. I'm your shopping buddy."

"No one could ever replace my sister." *Just like no one could ever replace my dad—Evanston Coleman.*

"What's her name? Maybe I can Google her on whitepages.com," Lindsay asked as she walked away to check out another item.

"Eva Jamieson. I hope she's listed."

"Consider it done," Lindsay assured her and for the next hour, they added more items to Kelsi's baby wish list.

Chapter

Eleven

Kidd got his stubbornness honestly—from his mother and maybe his father too, because neither he nor his mother had been the first to call after the blowup at Grandma BB's house.

Twelve days later and it seemed like every woman who carried the Jamieson name had snubbed him, including Grandma BB and there wasn't even a "j" in her name.

The Jamieson men, on the other hand, had plenty to say about his behavior. Finally, Ace invited—or rather summoned—him to lunch at Applebee's. Now, they were sitting across the table from each other, and Kidd watched Ace practically swallow his food without chewing. "You know you owe Momma an apology?" Ace said between munches on his fries.

"Yeah, I know." Kidd rubbed his neck and shifted his body in the booth. "But Ma lied to us," he defended in disbelief. "All this time I thought Samuel played her for a fool, which he did, but Ma *let* him."

"Get over it." Ace licked ketchup off his finger and picked up another fry. "She's still our mother."

Kidd had five years on Ace when it came to bonding with Samuel. Their father had been his hero. Resentment started to build when he was in grade school and other children had fathers show up for activities, and Kidd had to settle for his grandfather. Not only did girls need their daddies, but so did boys.

He continued to watch his brother devour his meal as if Talise didn't cook for him. Kidd snorted. Being a married man had matured Ace beyond belief. Salvation gave him an extra boost. "I am so not liking you right now ordering me around."

"Get over that too. Now, when are you going to stop by Mom's house?"

Since Kidd didn't like the silent treatment from family members, he would concede. "This evening."

"Good." Ace waved for the server as he gulped down his second glass of lemonade. "Please give my brother the check." He grinned.

That was his kid brother. Maturity was still a little ways off.

Hours later, like a boy accepting his punishment, Kidd measured his steps on the pathway to his mother's front door. As he rang the bell, he almost wished she wasn't home. That wish didn't come true as she fumbled with the locks and opened the door. There was no smile forthcoming or light in her eyes. She didn't even invite him inside. Folding her arms, she stared—no, glared—at him.

"Ma," he said and nodded.

"Kevin Lawrence," she stated his given and middle name.

Not a good sign. He exhaled. She wasn't going to make

this easy. "I'm sorry for what I said and how I acted. May I come in?"

She didn't move right away as she squinted. Finally, his mother widened the door and walked away. Kidd took that as an invite.

Usually Boston barked and raced toward him, but even the Yorkie blinked open his eyes and went back to sleep. Kidd closed the door and stuffed his hands in his pockets. On his drive there, he coaxed himself not to be judgmental when the Lord spoke to him.

Does not My Word say to honor your mother and your father, so that thy days will be long upon the earth? The Lord chastened him with Ephesians 6:2.

Kidd was ashamed, because he hadn't done either with his blowup toward his mom. He immediately repented. "I overreacted."

"You did more than that." Twirling around, she fixed her hands on her hips, then cast him a disapproving expression, one that he had seen many times as a teenager when he had made the wrong decision.

"I know." Kidd nodded. "I guess in my eyes, my mother can do no wrong," he admitted.

"Having two children without the benefit of marriage is wrong, and I repented for that."

"It's just that…" He paused, then glanced around the dwelling. "I blamed Samuel for everything. I grew up wanting to be your and Ace's hero. I wanted folks to know that nobody messed with my family unless they came through me," he said, pouring his heart out.

Sandra took a seat and stared into space. "I loved him from the beginning, no questions asked. Think what you want about me, son. I can accept that, but Raimond didn't deserve your attitude. I enjoyed his company." Her expression saddened and she fumbled with her fingers.

"You see, I gave up so much loving Samuel—missed career opportunities, a twenty-four-hour husband and father for my boys. God washed my sins away. He also redeemed Raimond with His blood and being with him…" Her eyes lit up. "It was like getting everything I had lost with your father return to me. My passion in life, carefree happiness, and much longed for companionship."

"I didn't know you were lone—" He thought about what Eva had said. Had his wife seen something that Kidd hadn't?

"It doesn't matter now. You have succeeded. Your heroics have chased a good man away. Raimond has enough going on in his life and he doesn't have room for any more drama." A tear fell and she didn't bother to wipe it away. "I will always love you, Kevin Jamieson, but at the moment I don't like your ways." She *tsk*ed. "How rooted are you in Christ, Kevin? You've been saved five-plus years. Yet, you still let the devil push your buttons. I advise you reread Matthew 13 and ask God to deepen your roots that your faith and peace in Him becomes unmovable." She stood and walked to the door. Without another word, she opened it.

Kidd blinked as he gulped for air. She was kicking him out? In all his years growing up and the shenanigans he'd put her through, his mother had been there through thick and thin and not once did his mother threaten to put him in the streets, which technically, she wasn't doing now, because he had a home to go to. He had survived without Samuel's love, but his Momma's? It was like dying a slow death. He kissed her cheek. "I love you, Mom, and I truly am sorry."

"I accept your apology." She closed the door.

In his car, Kidd sat there and stared at his mother's condo. Was this Raimond dude that important to her? She was letting another man come between them? But Raimond hadn't hurt her, Kidd had done it himself. For the first time in his life, Kidd realized his simple sorry wasn't going to restore their relationship. "Lord, I know You completely save. Help me not to let the devil pull my chain. In Jesus name. Amen."

Finally, with an achy heart, he started the ignition and headed toward home where he knew his wife wouldn't put him out. At least, she hadn't so far after they had the big blowup, following Grandma BB's party. Eva genuinely liked his mother, not as a daughter-in-law, but as a best friend.

"You are one selfish man, Kevin Jamieson!" Eva had fumed after they put Kennedy to bed. His wife knew how to get her point across without screaming or yelling. She could win a playing charades with little enough. Her body language, which included her evil eye, twisted lips, rolling her neck, and wagging her finger could convey any message.

Although they never went to bed angry, Kidd knew he couldn't chalk it up as bad behavior and go back to the way things used to be. He was ashamed of being ashamed.

When he walked through the garage to the kitchen, Eva must have sensed his mood, knowing he had stopped by his mother's. She gave him his space and held her tongue as she prepared his favorite meal.

If it wasn't for Kennedy's chatter, there wouldn't have been any conversation at the dinner table.

He cleaned the kitchen afterward then retreated to his man cave and closed the door under the guise of watching a sports program. Television couldn't provide the peace he craved.

Bowing his head, he cried out to the Lord, "Jesus, I know I've shamed You, myself, and insulted my mother."

Confess your sins for I am just and faithful to forgive. The Lord's Words seemed to embrace him.

So Kidd released the remnants that evidently he hadn't purged when God saved him years ago.

Your struggle is not against flesh and blood, but against the rulers, against the powers, against the world forces of this darkness, against the spiritual forces of wickedness in the heavenly places, God ministered to his heartache. *But you are overcome by My Spirit...*

His prayer time was cut short when he felt someone tap him on his leg and begin to climb on his lap. Although he wasn't ready to end his time with God, he welcomed God's gift—his daughter.

Kennedy smothered him with hugs and kisses at the same time telling him she was mad at him.

"Kami said women are 'posed to be mad," Kennedy blabbered. "But I don't want to be mad at you, Daddy."

Her innocence humbled him. When he realized what his daughter repeated, Kidd contemplated payback to the little girl who was growing up too fast. Parke's adopted daughter possessed the craftiness of the Jamiesons and she wasn't even a teenager yet.

"Daddy doesn't want you to be mad at him either." Kidd trapped her in his arms where they sat quietly. He continued to pray silently, rocking his daughter until she fell asleep. "God, You said I'm an overcomer. I will not yield to that temptation...anymore." He took a deep breath and carefully thought about what he was saying, essentially making a vow before God. Yes, he would battle that demon. "In Jesus name, Lord. Amen."

Getting to his feet, he kissed Kennedy's hair as he snuggled her close and walked into the bedroom that Eva and *his* mother had lovingly decorated. Eva joined him with a warm towel. Kidd watched as she removed Kennedy's clothes, washed her up, and then slipped on her pajamas without a stir from Kennedy.

With the task complete, Eva turned and gazed into his eyes. The night light cast a seductive glow on her face. "I love you, Kevin Jamieson," she whispered. Slipping her fingers through his, Eva led him out of Kennedy's bedroom to theirs. Behind closed doors, loving his wife was the best healing God had given him.

Chapter

Twelve

Sandra stopped counting the days since she last spoke with Raimond. The short time they had been inseparable seemed like a lifetime ago. She crossed one leg over her knee in the sitting area of a boutique, keeping an eye on the dressing room, waiting for her client to emerge. Shopping had always been her comfort zone and distraction, whether it was something for herself, family, or clients.

Anything could spark memories of Raimond, food, clothes, and other men. He had stamped a fingerprint on her heart and it was hard to smear it off. Although she missed Raimond, Sandra wasn't one of those women to beg a man to be with her, even if it was heartbreaking to be without him.

After Kidd's outright rudeness, Sandra couldn't blame Raimond for suggesting they step back and take care of the storms that were brewing in their lives, but she did blame him for giving up so easily. Wasn't she worth it? Didn't she deserve a man who would fight for her? Kidd was more bark than bite—most of the time. Of course, Raimond would never know that.

God knew she forgave her tenderhearted son who loved hard and would fight to the end for those he loved. Unfortunately, he had gone too far this time, because she was starting to fall in love again.

Sandra dismissed the whimsical notion and scanned the showroom stocked with styles and accessories to dress consumers of any age. Although she loved shopping for men, Sandra needed to steer clear of men's tie displays. When a gray- and-yellow strip tie and matching dress socks set caught her eye, Sandra had backtracked and envisioned Raimond pulling off the look.

Enough drifting! Sandra checked her bracelet watch. Her indecisive teenage client was trying on her fourth prom dress. The picky girl was one of the reasons why her doctor mother and attorney father had hired Sandra for the task. Their daughter flustered them—their words, not hers.

What a pity, because Sandra couldn't imagine not sharing those special moments with her granddaughters.

"Aisha?" Sandra called for the girl.

"Yes, ma'am?"

"Do you need any help?"

"Uh-uh."

Her parents would have corrected her to say *yes* or *no*, but Sandra was too preoccupied with other cares to do so. She leaned back and glanced over her shoulders and caught a glimpse of a teenage couple, holding hands and laughing as they passed by the store window. Sandra sighed. There was nothing that could compare with being in love. Her heart sunk as she replayed Raimond's final goodbye.

The Saturday of Grandma BB's birthday bash had been filled with so much passion from the moment Raimond picked her up. It felt so good to go to one of the Jamiesons' family function with a date and have them receive him with enthusiasm, minus Grandma BB and Kidd. The day held so many promises of more dating marathons, but as the sun set, Raimond escorted her home. There was no hand-holding, whispers, smiles, or conversation. They both rode quietly in their own thoughts.

Sandra had no idea what was to come when he walked her to the door. She had invited him in and attempted to apologize for her son's behavior.

In her living room, he didn't join her on the love seat. Raimond sat in an adjacent chair and reached for her hand. Looking into his eyes, the sadness was overwhelming. She didn't have the power or energy to 'kiss and make it better.'

"Sandra," he had started, *"I believe you are perfect for me..."*

She smiled. Without touching her lips, Raimond had dispatched a kiss in the air and it landed on its target. She felt it, and its warmth had engulfed her.

"And I told you I'd always be honest with you." He *inhaled and eyed Boston, who lay quietly at Sandra's feet, then exhaled. "I've caused enough discord in my life. Your son was really hurt by his father's betrayal as Kelsi was by mine. I can take her blows for just cause, but Kidd? You and he need to resolve some things. I want you in my life, but maybe our timing is off and our pace is too fast."*

No!!! Sandra had swallowed; her heart raced. She calmly and carefully stated, "I apologize for Kidd's behavior. He's a protector. I reared him better than that and God has been working on him."

"I'm sure you did, babe." His thumb rubbed her knuckles. *"But he's not spiritually healed,"* he said softly what her heart shouted. *"But family is important and I'm trying to play catch-up with the only child I have. If I'm going to be someone's mental punching bag, then I'm only getting in the ring with Kelsi. I need to put all my energies into fighting her demons. I can't slay Kidd's too."*

Sandra's heart had cracked. While she had admired Raimond's frankness in the beginning, at the moment, she didn't welcome it. They were barely three weeks into their "getting to know you phase" when she knew what was coming next. "So you're walking away?" She dared him to display his signature-crooked smile and tell her no, that she was jumping to conclusions.

"Let's agree to step back and take a break," he pleaded with a wounded animal expression.

Sandra willed herself not to react in a way that he could misinterpret as needy, so she didn't respond.

The man didn't want her. So what petition was she supposed to take to the Lord? *Make him want me.* God gave everyone free will and Raimond was exercising that. Okay. She took a deep breath. So she would have to deny her affections for Raimond and act professional while working with him as a client. *Sandra cleared her throat and straightened her body. "What about my involvement at the museum? I was looking forward to the fashion evolution display—that's what I started calling it."*

"Baby…"

Why did he have to call her that? Her resolve of keeping it professional slipped. He had only called her that endearment twice, earlier today at Grandma BB's party, and now.

"More than anything, I would like that. You have no idea how much, but you're too much of a temptation. My feelings for you grow so much stronger each day that I want to shut out the world for a secret place where no one would find us, but that's wishful thinking. My world has excluded Kelsi for too long. I failed her once, and I can't do it again.

"I understand," she said and stood. There was no use prolonging their goodbye. She walked to her door and opened it. He walked out without the confident swagger that made her smile.

The image vanished as Sandra's young client distracted her with her presence. Sandra's jaw dropped and she could only stare.

Aisha seemed pleased by her stunned expression. The red wine chiffon long dress had transformed this teenager into a princess. What a transformation. This moment made Sandra want to rush her granddaughters to grow up, because she couldn't wait to go prom shopping with them and their mothers.

Finally, a "wow" escaped and a "gorgeous" slipped from her mouth. While see-through garments seemed to be the latest craze, Sandra felt comfortable to recommend this dress. It gave the illusion that the midriff was bare. From the waist up to the heart-shaped strapless bodice, the dress was hand sewn with rhinestones. But Sandra had to do something about the girl's bare shoulders since Aisha had a voluptuous bust for her age.

"I like this one too, Miss Sandra," the girl said as she twirled around.

"But there are a few more accessories I would like to suggest."

The girl was already shaking her head in protest. Too bad. Sandra could dress anyone to perfection. "Right now, the dress outshines you." She stood and tapped her finger to her lips, considering bridal epaulettes. "Delicate jewelry draping your shoulders and teasing the top of the bodice would set it off."

The girl pouted, another *too bad*. The dress and the jewelry were pricey, but clients requested Sandra because she stayed within budget. She thought about Raimond again and the open line of credit he opened at several stores for her to shop for him. He probably closed it the same day he shut down their relationship.

Sandra forced herself to refocus. She still had to get Aisha's hair and makeup done, plus the shoes.

Sandra paid for the dress and they were off to their next stop, Plaza Frontenac Mall where she first met Raimond for dinner. As she and Aisha strolled past the restaurant, Sandra craned her neck to see the table they had shared, along with some of their secrets.

She swallowed and kept walking toward the designer shoe stores. This outing took a little longer and Aisha got her way on the heels. She dangled the shoes in one hand and gave her client a stern look. "Only if you agree to the ballerina slip-ons over there."

Aisha slumped.

"Believe me, you'll thank me for them later."

Their day of shopping ended soon after that when Sandra dropped Aisha off at her Ladue mansion. The next morning, Sandra would accompany Aisha and her mother to the salon for a test run style for Aisha's natural hair.

On the drive home, Raimond invaded her thoughts again.

It took years for Sandra to get Samuel out of her system. She prayed that Raimond would be a faded memory sooner rather than later.

Saturday morning, Kidd had been out of the shower five minutes when somebody, probably Ace, laid their finger on the doorbell and didn't let up. Eva and his daughter had already left to meet his mother to baby shop. Finally decent, Kidd went to answer it.

Spying through the peephole, Parke's mugshot was magnified before his eyes. Kidd groaned as he opened the door. His cousin nudged his way inside.

"I believe my name is on the deed to this property," Kidd warned, playing hardball, to irritate Parke, which never worked.

"Congratulations." His cousin grinned. "I have a deed to property that I believe you were my guest for an extended-extended stay."

Kidd grunted. He hated when Parke upped him. "Right, but my wife could be indecent."

"Your wife told my wife to tell me that's it's all clear over here." Strolling into Kidd's living room, Parke made himself at home. After claiming a spot on the sofa, he stretched his legs. "Listen, this is a courtesy call from your Jamieson cousins." He folded his arms and so did Kidd as he leaned against the door frame and waited for whatever the Jamiesons men deemed necessary this time of morning. He had come to learn in this family that courtesy calls meant they were up in your business whether you wanted advice or not.

"Some men think with their pants."

"I'm not in that group," Kidd argued. "I'm faithful—"

Parke cut him off. "True, but you think with your tongue. I can quote you all kinds of Scriptures about the unruly tongue, the boastful tongue, but the point is we can't perfect our walk with Christ without taming the thing."

He didn't like Parke's judgment call, even if his cousin was right. "That's *my* problem—"

"Which we've made our problem. The Jamiesons are your brother's keeper."

"I appreciate that, but I'm grown," Kidd reminded him.

"So is your mother."

"That's different."

"Is it? If this Raimond guy had turned out to be a jerk, he would have had to contend with the J-Force of all the Jamiesons: me, Malcolm, Cameron, your brother, and don't think the women would stay on the sideline. Grandma BB would probably call her Red Hat society ladies for backup and I know some of them pack."

"Yes, how can I forget," Kidd said, thinking about the tongue-lashing Cheney, Hallison and their friend, Imani, gave him when he first arrived in St. Louis, then he heard about Grandma BB's trial on assault charges with the ladies in red flooding the courtroom.

"See, cuz. We've had Sandra's back as if she was a Jamieson legally. Put up the kid gloves—pun intended." Parke grinned.

"Funny."

"Seriously, this is the time to pray for her. The way you showed out in front of Raimond would make him doubt that the Lord saved you. You can put major fear in a man by saying very little."

"I apologized to Momma." He stood taller and rubbed his eyes. "I can't believe I really hurt her. But if Raimond Mayfield scares that easily and runs away—" he snapped his fingers, "—like that, then he wasn't man enough for her."

Parke nodded. "Now, I agree with you there, but I think Sandra is a good judge of character. We don't know what the man was going through and you owe him an apology too."

"I know," Kidd mumbled and stuffed his hands in his pockets. "Well, I heard he's working at some new black history museum in the Central West End. I plan to go see him."

Parke invited himself to tag along.

"Not necessary. I'll be on my best behavior." The way he had been praying, repenting, and reading his Bible, Kidd trusted God to help him bridle his words.

"I know. I'm going to make sure of that." Parke stood and glanced out the window. He gave a thumbs up. "And so are they."

Kidd peeped out the window. "Figures," he griped.

Unlike his other estranged siblings, with the exception of his baby sister, Queen, courtesy of his philandering father, the St. Louis Jamiesons were a die-hard bunch. They were tough-loved whether Kidd wanted them or not.

Still, Kidd would rather not have an audience when he humiliated himself in front of Raimond.

Hours later, after a day of running errands for their wives, to Kidd's relief, by the time they all made it to The Heritage House museum, it was closed. That gave him more time to practice his spiel of remorse.

Chapter

Thirteen

"My morning sermon is found in Psalm 18. Verse thirty sums it up, God's way is perfect," Pastor Rouse told his Temple Church of Christ congregation. "So stop getting in His way by doing it your way."

My way, Raimond repeated as he scanned the passage, beginning at verse one. Wasn't reconciling with Kelsi God's perfect way?

What about Sandra? His mind demanded an answer. After all, didn't God lead him toward her too?

Raimond cringed when he thought about the way he bowed out of his relationship with Sandra. What a coward! In hindsight, he guessed he could have done it better.

He forced his mind to concentrate on the sermon, because he needed comfort from the Lord. Although Raimond had been attending this church since he relocated to St. Louis, only once could he say he felt complete and that was the one Sunday Sandra had come with him. It only took one time for her presence to be missed every time he stepped foot inside Temple Church of Christ. Yet, without her next to him with her worn Bible, the space felt void, even if there were others on the pew with him.

"This chapter is more than about reassurance of deliverance from our physical enemies. Often times, the torment comes in a spiritual battle first, then escalates to physical scrimmages. This doesn't have to upset your world, if you stay in God's plan," he said sternly. "I guess the next thing you might say, 'What is God's plan?' If you don't know, ask God. He designed your blueprints…"

Pastor Rouse preached for almost an hour, citing examples of Scriptures pointing to God's plan. He ended his sermon with an altar call for those with a repenting spirit. "Our ministers are here to pray for you, not to hear your sins. The Lord has already heard them. If you want your sins washed away, we have the water baptism in Jesus' name on standby. Afterward, if you want the power to keep you from falling, the Holy Ghost awaits, then you and Jesus will have a private heavenly conversation as evidence that you are filled with a power from God, not man. Won't you come?"

The congregation watched as several made their way down the aisle in response to Pastor Rouse's plea.

Soon, the offering was taken and the pastor gave the benediction. Raimond greeted a few members and then headed to the parking lot with a burning question, "God, what is Your plan for me, Kelsi, and Sandra?"

God didn't give him a private consultation, so for the next few days, Raimond meditated on God's Word while submitting to Kelsi's terms—stubbornness she had inherited from her mother—and had not called her again until God gave him the game plan for his next move.

When Townsend called one morning, Raimond gave him an update on his personal and professional status; his friend disagreed with Raimond's decision to cave in to Kelsi's demands.

But Raimond had little choice other than remain in a holding pattern with his daughter until God orchestrated the next move. This is when he wished he could take back what he said to Sandra. "We have kindred spirits, broken pasts, and passions that haven't fostered. Man, I wish you would've met her, because she was something special."

Of course, Townsend had an opinion on that too. Actually, his friend seemed to be amused. "This coming from a reformed womanizer—your words, not mine."

"Words that I said more than ten years ago," Raimond practically snapped, then calmed down. "Will you forget some of the things I said—please?"

"Rai, you know I'm on your side. Before you left, you're the one who reminded me to help keep you focused. That's all I'm doing."

"I know." Raimond nodded. He couldn't fault the man for trying to ease his burden, even though his counsel was way off base. It had been a big move with a big mission. "Sometimes I've wondered if Ivy lured me back only to taunt me with Kelsi's rejection. Before Christ, I was too arrogant to beg, but after Jesus saved me, it seems humility has been stamped on my forehead along with footprints of people who I've allowed to walk over me, including Sandra's son. It took all the Holy Ghost within me to tame my tongue and fist."

His nostrils flared just thinking about it. "I'm not one to tolerate disrespect from another man, and especially a younger one who could be my son."

"Ah… I thought we were talking about Kelsi."

Busted. "Ah, right. We were, I don't know how Sandra's son slipped into our conversation."

"You fell hard for her." Townsend was quiet and Raimond wondered what he was thinking. "Didn't you say God had a plan?"

Townsend was listening. Raimond smirked.

"Maybe Sandra's not part of it."

Or maybe not. Raimond didn't want to hear that. "Maybe it's time for me to go. I have a museum to open." They ended the call.

A few hours later, the hairs on Raimond's back tickled and he flexed his muscles as footsteps approached him from behind. He and Dace stopped scrutinizing an art piece and turned around to see Kidd clearing the doorway with his cousins close behind.

He groaned and mumbled, "Not today."

Dace must have picked up on Raimond's tension as they both watched their visitors' every move. Technically, the museum wasn't open, but they welcomed onlookers to come in and see their progress. "You know I pack. It's your call." He hissed under his breath.

Right. Raimond nodded slowly. He would have to talk to Dace about not carrying guns and knives at the museum, even if Missouri was a conceal-and-carry gun state. Plus, post that sticker at the door for visitors not to bring weapons on his premises. The only guns Raimond wanted on his property were wax replicas. "Nah. I'm only concerned about the big guy in the front." He refused to be disrespected again.

"Dude, they're all big, but I got your back. D.C. ain't for sissies."

Raimond met Kidd halfway as the others began to snoop around. "Young man, you're on my property and I could have you charged with trespassing, if you've come to make any trouble."

"That won't be necessary, because I came to apologize," he stated. But his face held no expression, so Raimond didn't relax just yet.

They stared at each other and Raimond could see hints of Sandra in her son's eyes. "How's Sandra?"

"You shouldn't have to ask." Kidd folded his arms. "If you really cared about my mother, you would have fought for her."

Raimond twisted his lips and looked to Dace who feigned putting the finishing touches on the African King and Queen pieces, but Raimond knew he was biding time, waiting for a signal to act as a bouncer.

"You have no idea what's going on in my life. If I have to deal with drama, it will be from my daughter who I'm trying to reconnect with. I'm only trying to plead my case with her."

Kidd grunted. "So you deserted her too." He shook his head in disgust.

Yeah, Raimond was disgusted with a lot of things the old Raimond did too, but those things were nailed on the cross and he wouldn't let anyone yank them down and dangle them before his eyes.

"You're giving me more reasons not to like you," Kidd said tensely.

"I only need Sandra's permission to date her," Raimond reminded him. "And that was a hard decision to say, 'let's step back,' but I'm not your father. I have my own burdens, so I hope you'll understand why I won't carry your weight too, on my shoulders. I can't answer for your father's sins, only mine. I did, then God forgave me. Give your hurts to God."

Surprisingly, those words had an effect on Kidd as the tension seemed to dissipate between them. Kidd looked away with an expression of uncertainty as if he was unsure of himself. "I thought I had."

"Then leave it on the cross." Raimond was about to say more, but one of the other men walked up. Nudging Kidd to the side, the man stuck out his hand. "I'm not sure if you remember me from Grandma BB's party. Parke Jamieson." He tilted his head. "His cousin."

"Sorry, I don't recall, but it's nice to meet you." Raimond nodded. "I hope you will come back when we officially open."

"I wouldn't miss it." Parke's eyes lit with excitement. "Hey, I noticed you have a copy of *The Negro Motorist Green-Book.*"

"Yes, the Smithsonian had extra copies, so the one in the case is actually on loan from them."

"Ahh. The Smithsonian," Parke repeated. "I can get lost in their African American history section." He grinned and shook his head. "My father talked about books my grandfather used when he traveled. After Grandpa P's death, a lot of his stuff was lost or sold before my father could retrieve them."

"We find history's treasures at estates sales or on eBay all the time. Plus, we do receive donations from the deceased families' loved ones." Raimond folded his arms.

Kidd cleared his throat, reminding Raimond and Parke of his presence. "Only out of curiosity, what's the deal with this green book?"

"I'll show you." Raimond gave Dace a signal with his hand that everything was under control.

Parke seemed to be enthralled with the mansion's architecture as the cousins trailed him. "This place is airy and has a historic feel to it."

"Yes." Raimond veered behind the staircase that exposed another area. "We have eight very large rooms on this floor and when they're finished, each exhibit will have different themes. *The Negro Motorist Green-Book* is only a small piece of memorabilia in our travel room, which features African Americans who made history in transportation from the horse and buggy to space travel." Slipping his hands into his pockets, Raimond waited while the two examined the items that were already set up.

"There will also be a sports room, vintage black toys, and copies of the first black publications."

"That sounds great, Raimond," Parke said. "St. Louis is a big sports town with legends like Lou Brock, Bob Gibson, Ozzie Smith, and countless others."

Peering through an enclosed box-shaped glass on a pedestal, Raimond pointed to the pages. "This is it. The travel book for blacks published by a man named Victor Green. 'Driving while black' isn't a new term. Being black on the road during the Jim Crow era was challenging and sometimes dangerous, depending where you stopped. As you can see, it lists where blacks could eat, sleep, and see entertainment with the same dignity as whites. After thirty years, the last book was printed in 1964. I guess Green thought the Civil Rights Act would put an end to discrimination, but the book could be updated today to include sundown towns."

"Some of those places remain all-white to date after

running blacks out of town decades ago," Parke added.

"I see you know your history." Raimond grinned. It was refreshing to find a kindred spirit with someone who loved the black history in American history.

"Triple AAA for black folks...humph, humph, humph." Kidd shook his head. "I get the hotels, restaurants, beauty and barber shops, gas stations, and entertainment spots, but tourist homes?"

Raimond answered without waiting for him to finish. "It listed housing along the road like cabins for colored people or Mrs. S. H. Smith opening her private homes for African Americans who were turned down at other establishments."

Kidd seemed to be in thought, so Raimond gave him time to digest his new found history. "And whites can't understand the rage, hate, and mistrust black folks have."

"It's important to remember that all whites weren't racists and I can give you countless examples like the Grimke sisters, Sarah and Angeline. They were born into a slaveholding family and so abhorred the institution that they moved to the North and became sympathetic to our ancestors' plight and became abolitionists," Raimond explained.

"Don't forget that some whites were just as afraid of racists too, because they could suffer backlash for trying to help our kinfolks," Parke added.

"You're right." Finally, Raimond walked ahead. "As you can see, priceless artifacts aren't limited to coins, art, and stamps. The enclosures not only serve as security, but more importantly, temperature control. I have an extensive background in historic preservation. Most paper products made before the 1980s used acetate. When it interacts with oxygen, it begins to disintegrate with the slightest touch.

Today's material, especially photos, are digital and so there's little worry about physical preservation. Pictures posted on the web will allow things to last until Jesus comes back.

Parke twisted his mouth and put his hands on his waist. "The genealogists in my family have been collecting documents for decades, but we never thought about what not to do—not using glue or tape on the back of pictures, even though we dated them, before storing them in plastic protected photo albums. We have my tenth great-grandmother's journals from the mid-1880s and they're about to fall apart."

"Air temperature is crucial for protection," Raimond stated. "I would love to take a look at them and offer suggestions." He rubbed his hands together, ending the impromptu tour. "Everything will fall in place for the official opening, which will be on Juneteenth, the day that celebrates—"

"We know about Juneteenth. My cousin makes sure of that. We're tenth generation descendants of a royal African tribe."

Parke cleared his throat. "I'm tenth. You're eleventh. I've upped you on a generation."

"Whatever." Kidd shoved his cousin.

Raimond was amused by their camaraderie. It seemed like Parke had a calming effect on Kidd.

"I'll see if I have anything I can donate, and I would love to volunteer. Maybe I can run some ideas by you."

"Hold up." Kidd frowned at Parke. "Whose side are you on?"

"The Lord's side," his cousin answered and slapped Kidd on the shoulder. "Your mission is complete here. You've apologized. Let's go before you say something and have to apologize again."

"My cousin is right," Kidd surprisingly agreed, then became quiet. "Since you've made your decision concerning my mother, we have nothing else to discuss." With a nod, Kidd whistled for the others who had dispensed to do some unaccompanied exploring on their own.

Raimond said his goodbyes and watched them leave. *Sandra.* He was a jerk when it came to relationships years ago and it seemed like he was still a jerk when it came to a very special woman. If Kidd could man up and apologize, so could Raimond, because he wasn't happy without her.

Chapter

Fourteen

Kelsi was in her last trimester and couldn't be happier. Surrounded by family and friends for her shower, Kelsi admired Lindsay's handiwork.

Her sister had outdone herself in the decorations for her baby shower. Besides the names on the list Kelsi gave her, Lindsay had tracked down friends from Kelsi's childhood, high school, and even some of her long-lost sorority sisters.

Stephan's mother, grandmother, and aunts were just as excited as women from her side of the family. Out of nowhere, she wondered about the Mayfields she had never met. They never reached out after Raimond's defection, so Kelsi knew very little about them. Since they had been out of sight, they had been out of her mind most of her life.

Happy thoughts, she reminded herself. Thinking about anything and anyone associated with Raimond always turned her mood sour.

Kelsi took a deep breath, rubbed her belly, which made

her smile, then concentrated on those who were present to help her celebrate.

Bloodhound Lindsay had even tracked down Eva Jamieson, to Kelsi's delight. The two pregnant mommies brushed bellies as they hugged like old friends when Eva walked through the door.

Not surprisingly, Eva's persona was something Kelsi wanted to emulate as a young mother, especially after learning they were less than a year apart with Eva being the oldest.

Eva made being a young mother look easy. *She must have a loving husband like my Stephan,* Kelsi surmised. She made maternity clothes look like the next fashion trend and so effortless that Kelsi craved it.

"I love that powder blue on you," Kelsi complimented Eva's attire. She could see herself in that color, complementing her brown skin tone as it had with Eva's fair skin with a dust of freckles.

"Thanks, my mother-in-law chose it." Eva beamed. "While we were shopping—her favorite thing to do—she saw this ensemble and told me if I didn't buy it, she would and she'd bill my husband." They giggled.

"Awww, I have the sweetest mother-in-law too, but I wouldn't want her to shop for me." Kelsi glanced over her shoulder and winked at Mrs. Lana Edwards who seemed to be amused by their conversation.

"My daughter-in-law tells the truth," she said. With her white hair swept up in a bun, she looked like the lovable grandma she was soon to become. "I'm not a shopper, but I definitely need to update my wardrobe."

Eva beamed. "Well, I'll have to pass on my mother-in-law's number. She's a personal fashion shopper."

Mrs. Edwards perked up. "Please do!"

"She may have two new clients," Kelsi added, before Lindsay got the party underway.

After introductions were made and guests congratulated Eva on her pregnancy, Eva seemed to fit right in with Kelsi's longtime friends.

For the next hour, everyone was subjected to baby topics while they feasted on gourmet sandwiches, fruits, and treats.

"Time to open the gifts," Lindsay announced as if they were on a time schedule.

Kelsi shifted in the recliner designed at the party baby seat. Where Eva's mother-in-law was a fashion expert, Lindsay was a time management connoisseur.

There were so many boxes, big and small, but Kelsi eyed Eva's gift basket that she rolled in when she arrived. She bided her time, not wanting to be partial to the other nice presents she received. Besides, she had to wait impatiently for Lindsay to hand over the next gift and make sure their mother kept a meticulous list of the givers. The generosity of her guests was overwhelming. Even her baby stretched and seemed to squirm with excitement.

When Lindsay rolled Eva's gift to her, guests *ooh*ed and *ahh*ed over the square blue wicker basket on wheels with a cartoon emblem. It was the size of a small laundry basket and had a big satin bow tied around it. Kelsi and the others were surprised that the bow was actually a lightweight baby blanket.

"I have one of those," Eva explained. "It's great when you don't want to carry a diaper bag while wearing that cute baby carrier you just got."

"Great gift," echoed among the guests.

"I love it!" Kelsi reached over and hugged her new friend. "When did you get it?"

"I'm a crafty type of person, so I went crazy shopping, then my mother-in-law helped me put it together."

"I've got to meet this mother-in-law," Kelsi said.

"She's hosting our ladies tea in July. I'm sure she won't mind me bringing you. We've all brought guests from time to time."

"Great. Little Stephan isn't due till mid-August, so I would love to come before I get on mommy duty."

Eva appeared as happy as Kelsi felt when she accepted.

Once all the gifts and cards were opened, guests gathered their things to leave. Some were encouraged to carry plates home, because of the amount of food that was left.

Although Kelsi was tired and ready for a nap, she was glad that Eva lingered longer and gushed over some of the outfits for Stephan. "I'm so glad you came."

Eva hugged her. "Thanks for going through the trouble of inviting me."

"No trouble." Lindsay waved from across the room. "You and your husband were listed in whitespages.com."

"Okay, Mommy-to-be, I think we both need a nap, so I'm going home." Eva stood. "And, Lindsay, consider this your personal invite to attend the ladies tea with Kelsi. It's intimate. Gloves, hats, and pearls are required."

"Ooh." Kelsi couldn't wait. Standing in the doorway, she waved as Eva drove off.

"I like her," Lindsay said after closing the door behind Eva.

"Me too. I should have added her mother-in-law to my guest list. She sounds really nice."

"Yes, she does. Now, why don't you rest while we straighten up."

"No argument from me." Kelsi yawned, then headed down the hall to her master bedroom, then stopped. "Oh, tomorrow, we should go shopping."

Lindsay put her fists on her hips. "You've got to be kidding. You won't need anything for months."

Kelsi laughed. "For pearls, gloves, and hats, silly."

Soft kisses woke Kelsi from her nap. Smiling, she stretched and opened her eyes.

"What store—no, *stores*—did your guests buy out?" Stephan joked. His light brown eyes twinkled as he gathered her in his arms and nuzzled her neck. "Did you have a good time?"

Kelsi cooed, "I did! The gifts, guests, and food were exceptional. By the way, our mothers packed away leftovers, including a plate for you."

"Found it." He gave her a boyish grin.

He was so adorable when he had/spotted a mischievous glint in his eyes. Kelsi hoped their son had his father's features, especially his smile and long lashes. And when Stephan Junior would become a man, he would probably have sculptured muscles like his athletic father. In a few years, they could try for a girl…like Eva's. She rubbed his smooth jaw and grinned herself.

"Sorry to wake you—" his husky voice betrayed him, "—but I missed my wife. I can only hang out with your baby brother for so long." Scooting her over, he climbed into the bed next to her.

She snuggled closer. Maybe, now that he was home, she could go back to sleep and this time she wouldn't dream about her father—Raimond, not Evan. Lately, when she least expected, Raimond's deep voice started to creep into her head. Her only memory of them was that of a five year-old and it was that image that appeared in her dreams.

Of course, if she really wanted to see an updated photo of Raimond, she could probably find his profile on LinkedIn, or other social media sites, but to do that would mean she was interested about him, which she wasn't.

A light snore caused Kelsi to look at her husband. Stephan's eyes were closed. "Babe?"

He stirred, but didn't open his eyes. "Umm?"

"Do you think I should reach out to Raimond? For the baby's sake," she quickly added.

His eyes popped open and he stared at her. She could tell he was thinking before he shrugged. "Sweetheart, our baby will be fine either way. What about you?" He stroked her cheek and she wanted to purr.

She squeezed her lips, considering her answer. Kelsi never fudged the truth with her husband. "I don't know. The little girl in me wants to kick, scream, and go on a temper tantrum for his disappearing act. His desertion caused me to blame myself for some imaginary thing I did."

"And what about the beautiful woman you've become?" He smiled. "I want whatever makes you happy. If he's only going to upset you, then I'll be the firewall." He patted his chest. Then he cracked his knuckles as his wedding band sparkled. "I'm sure Tyler will want to be in on the action too. Since lifting weights, your brother thinks he's one of the Avengers."

Kelsi chuckled. Her baby brother made her look like the baby with his height and build. Add his jet-black beard and it added to his maturity of a twenty-nine year-old. He was years past being a baby as he often reminded her. Of the three siblings, Tyler had the perfect silky light brown skin. Acne never afflicted him and with all his bumps and bruises, none had marred his handsome face. Tyler might be the youngest, but he would beat a man down over his older sisters.

Yes, Raimond would be met with double trouble, Kelsi thought, tickled by her husband working himself into a frenzy on her behalf. When he realized that he was the source of her amusement, Stephan laughed with her. "Sorry, but I take it personal when it comes to you."

"I love you for loving me so much." She shifted her body as the baby began to move and placed Stephan's hand on her stomach. It was a moment frozen in time as they witnessed God's miracle of life. Once their baby quieted, they shared a compassionate kiss. After a few pecks, Kelsi's lids fluttered. The moment was sweet and relaxing until a blurry image of Raimond seemed to be standing on the sideline, knocking on the door of her mind. Rolling her eyes, Kelsi sighed, tired of the mental harassment. "I don't know. Maybe I'll call him."

"Okay, babe." Stephan nodded, closed his eyes, then drifted off again as Kelsi contemplated when she would make that call to a stranger who fathered her. But what could he say and what did she want to hear?

It took more than a week before Kelsi made up her mind that today would be the day and she informed Stephan.

"Sweetheart, if he upsets you at all, he and I will have a talk. All right?" Stephan didn't crack a smile. Then he gave her a hug and lingering kiss before he left for the high school.

That afternoon after work, Kelsi gnawed her lips, debating. Stephan had already texted twice, asking for an update and reminding her she didn't owe Raimond anything.

I know, she texted back. How would their conversation begin and end? There wasn't enough time in her lifetime to play catch-up. Oddly, she whispered a prayer before tapping his number.

Her baby squirmed as she waited for Raimond to answer. Kelsi was so nervous as she counted the series of rings. "I hope I don't go into labor," she mumbled. If it went to voice mail, she would disconnect and take that as an omen.

"Hello?"

Kelsi's heart pounded. Her voice caught in her throat. What should she say first?

"Kelsi," he said, this time, with eagerness in his voice.

She swallowed and practiced her Lamaze breathing, then feign emotional and mental control. "Hello, Raimond. I'm returning your call."

"It's so good to hear your voice." He paused as if waiting for her response. She didn't have one and he must have sensed that as he cleared his throat. "Ah, I'm sorry for not being there for you. I hope you will forgive me…and maybe give me a chance to get to know my daughter again—"

"*Your* daughter?" she balked. "My name is Kelsi Coleman Edwards. My father is Evan Coleman who wiped away my tears, put me through college, and walked me down the aisle…" Her vision began to blur. Why was she getting so upset? She sniffed to capture the tears, then exhaled. "Now, he and my mother are eagerly awaiting their first grandchild."

"Kelsi Marie, I moved back to St. Louis for you."

What right does he have to use my middle name? "And

you moved away from me to be with every woman who crossed your path." He was quiet, so she lit into him with no mercy to spare. "Go back to your women, Raimond. There is nothing here for you...unless there's another woman."

"No," he said quietly, almost choking. "My move, my calls, and the museum I'm opening are all about you."

He made it sound like she was his world and Kelsi knew that wasn't the case. "And how could that be, since ladies are your weakness?"

"Sin was my weakness. I changed when I totally submitted myself to Jesus. I repented and was baptized in Jesus' name and just like the Bible says in Acts, He filled me with the Holy Ghost. I'm a new person." He paused. "Kelsi, my past is gone."

"That's funny." Instead of a mocking laugh, Kelsi found herself snarling. "Your past is constantly present in my head," she argued.

"It doesn't have to be, if you give me a chance. I'm sorry I didn't make you and your mother a priority, but I'm willing to make your child—my grandchild—a priority. You're all I have left, Kelsi."

"That's not my fault, Raimond. You were a rotten husband and a terrible father, so you don't have a good track record for being a good step-grandfather. Evan would be considered his grandfather." Where was all this bitterness coming from? Her parents had taught her to be respectable and courteous, but the man on the other end of this phone brought out the worst in her. She didn't need this stress. "Let me talk to my husband. Maybe after my son is born—"

"A boy?" Raimond's voice shook with such awe that Kelsi thought he was going to cry.

"Yes, Stephan and I are having a boy. Maybe when he's older, we'll talk." She was about to tap End Call when he yelled, "Wait!"

"I can understand if you're not ready for a one-on-one meeting, but my reasons for coming back home are genuine. The Heritage House Museum opens in two weeks. I would love for you and your husband to be my guests. Maybe we can start over by you seeing firsthand how I've changed."

"We'll think about it." This time she did disconnect. She rolled on her side and rubbed her tummy. She wasn't trying to be pulled into Raimond's world. The phone call was supposed to be about shutting him out of hers.

This isn't about you, a tiny voice scolded her.

She blinked and trembled, not sure where that voice came from.

Chapter

Fifteen

Two weeks later, against her better judgment, Kelsi arrived at The Heritage House Museum for its grand opening. Not only did Stephan accompany her as her bodyguard, her parents and siblings insisted on being there too, since it was a public event and they didn't need an invitation.

Stephan loosened his hold on Kelsi's hand and wrapped his arm around her. When she leaned into Stephan, he kissed her ear. "I've never seen a more beautiful pregnant lady than my wife. I like you in that color."

Kelsi giggled. She'd thought so since seeing Eva sport a similar shade of blue at her baby shower. She looked into those brown mesmerizing eyes that attracted her to him. "You've been saying that since the first day Dr. Taylor confirmed I was expecting."

"And I'll keep saying it." He gently rubbed her expanding womb. "Now, are you sure about this? I have no problem going back home."

Her heart fluttered. She was one blessed woman. "I'm not sure about anything at this moment, but I want to get this over with."

Taking her hand, Stephan nodded. "Then let's go."

The museum was housed in a mansion with a majestic entrance that enticed curious outsiders to come inside. Soft music greeted them as Stephan opened the door for her. Straining her ear, Kelsi searched for the source to see a live African American male quartet tucked in a corner, serenading the guests. Their presence had such a soothing effect on her nerves that she actually relaxed. A handful of staffers, dressed in period costumes and with ready smiles, welcomed them, then gave a brief overview of the museum's themed exhibits.

"Enjoy," the young woman said before moving on to the next group of newcomers with the spiel.

Kelsi craned her neck. An artsy person by nature, she was impressed, but her purpose was to meet her father—no, Raimond—she corrected herself.

"See him?" Stephan whispered, squeezing her hand.

She was about to shake her head, then she squinted. A good-looking gentleman came into her view. He held a group of other men captive with whatever tales he was weaving. There was something commanding about him. Could that be Raimond? At that moment, the man in question turned and made eye contact with her. Recognition draped his face.

Stephan was still looking around when the man excused himself and began a confident stride in her direction. He kept his smile in place as he greeted, nodded, and weakly shook hands en route. Spellbound, Kelsi couldn't move or speak, but her heart was pounding in her chest.

"Is that your father—I mean, *him*?" Stephan asked, breaking the trance.

Kelsi couldn't answer. Her memories of him were sketchy.

"Yes, that's Raimond Mayfield," her mother's voice echoed somewhere behind her.

Then Raimond's steps slowed, then faltered before stopping within feet of her. "Kelsi." His baritone voice was unmistakable and unforgettable.

Wow. Her mother had good taste, but terrible judgment. He was very handsome. She could only imagine how thirty plus years earlier he used his looks to his advantage. She nodded and he exhaled. "Thank you for coming," he said.

Kelsi said nothing. She couldn't open her mouth. She barely blinked, trying to reconcile that the man who stood before her was once her daddy.

Stephan broke the trance she was in by offering a handshake. "Hello, I'm Stephan Edwards, Kelsi's husband." Their greeting was warm.

"Ivy," Raimond spoke to her mother. Their exchange was cordial, even with her dad.

"Tyler." Her brother came to her side with a fierce look that had scared away many of her boyfriends, and age never made a difference with her younger brother. He had the body of a linebacker. Next, Tyler introduced Lindsay, as if their sister didn't have a quick tongue of her own.

Kelsi still hadn't found her voice by the time he glanced at her again. "Well, please help yourself to some light refreshments and walk about and check out the exhibits. Maybe, before you leave, we can chat?" he said with a hopeful expression.

She couldn't commit to anything at the moment and her family must have sensed her discomfort.

"You've done a great job," her father and mother said in unison, coming to her rescue.

Feeling her baby squirm, Kelsi gently stroked her stomach. The gesture caused Raimond to focus on her bulge. A crestfallen look flashed on his face, but he recovered when someone called his name.

"Duty calls for me to mingle, so please…spare me a few minutes of your time before you leave." He didn't wait for a response as he met a couple halfway, all smiles.

"Babe?" Stephan's voice brought her back to a familiar place.

Coming face-to-face with Raimond somehow felt foreign to Kelsi, as if she was meeting any man off the street. For her to greet Raimond with the hugs, smiles, and laughs, it would mean that all was forgotten. Well, she wasn't ready to sing Auld Lang Syne.

After reassuring her family that she was all right, they left her in the hands of her husband as they looked around. "Princess," her dad called. His hand was wrapped around her mother's. "We won't be far, but your mom and I are going to explore this place." After kissing her cheek, he was about to walk away, but stopped. "Don't be afraid to be you. You'll always be my daddy's little girl."

"Thank you, Daddy." Kelsi's eyes misted. He was a man she could depend on—always.

"I want you off your feet as much as possible." Stephan steered her toward a room set up like a theater and guided her to a row in the back, then sat next to her. Taking her hand, Stephan pulled her closer as they watched a series of film compilations entitled Riot for Rights.

The clips created 3-D images in Kelsi's mind. Although she had the basic understanding of black history, the pictures opened a new world: slave revolts and the force removal of Native Indians from their land. Then there were the racial riots in North Tulsa, Oklahoma, where more than a thousand businesses were burned down to the ground by a white mob.

Kelsi frowned at the magnitude of such hate. She had heard tidbits about the event referred to as Black Wall Street, but never had an image to validate it. So many emotions ran through her mind as she viewed the remnants of what was successful black wealth. The caption across the screen flashed: *Ten thousand blacks left homeless.*

Racism. *Why?* Kelsi gritted her teeth in disgust. Another day in black American history happened literally five minutes over the Mississippi River from downtown St. Louis, Missouri: East St. Louis, Illinois race riots.

Again, whites went on a rampage. Forty African Americans were killed and hundreds of thousands of properties were destroyed, all because blacks worked at a factory that whites wanted to picket. Another caption read: *Men, women, and children were beaten, stabbed, hanged, and burned.*

Then the images faded to a large number of children in New York City all dressed in white, marching in a silent protest against the East St. Louis riots.

"Wow, that was in 1917," Kelsi whispered.

Stephan tugged at the hairs in his mustache, a habit he did when thinking. "Yeah, and it was considered the first massive African American protest in America," Stephan read the sub titles, then shook his head. "Two wars were going on at the same time. World War I in Europe and a race war in America."

Most of the clips weren't longer than five minutes and the documentary had concluded. "We're bringing our son into a world of hate." She rubbed her stomach. "I'm scared."

She thought about the recent riots in Ferguson, Missouri. This time the destruction came by the hands of blacks in protest of a white officer. That incident was current. People across the world, whites, Asians, Palestinians, and others marched in solidarity with African American or police brutality. Sometimes, it was a toss-up.

A young man strolled from a corner and stood in the center of the room. He cleared his throat as he linked his hands. Introducing himself as Trent, he reminded her of a college professor with his neat appearance and wired glasses and rigid stance.

"I know these images are hard to digest, but Mr. Mayfield would like to leave visitors with two footnotes: Although whites perpetrated these acts, all whites aren't racists. That is important to remember, because some lost their lives along with blacks like Freedom Riders James Zwerg, Winonah Myers, and Joan Trumpower…Civil Rights Activist Viola Gregg Liuzzo and more, ladies and gentlemen. There is also a Christian outlook." He paused as both blacks and whites who were sitting in the room quietly waited for his reasoning. "We are not to hate those who hate us, but to pity them, because they don't know Christ. Blacks haven't been the only ones to trust God to deliver them out of slavery—the Jews suffered also, as well as other ethnic groups. And the sad part is slavery still exists today, along with sex trafficking. When will it all end, you may ask?" Trent scanned the audience. "When Jesus returns."

"Until then, we're stuck in this evil world with no hope,"

Kelsi mumbled. "I wish Jesus would do something now."

"I hear ya, babe." Stephan became quiet. "As fearless as I am, this type of hate is scary to me and we're going to need as much help as we can to survive. Maybe we should join a church for little Stephan's sake."

"Yeah." Kelsi played with her curls as others walked into the room and took their seats with no idea of what they were about to see. She turned to Stephan. "You know, it sounds so strange to put Raimond and God in the same sentence. He wasn't thinking about God when he was doing his dirt. What happened to make him change? If he's really changed." Kelsi shifted in her chair.

"Are you comfortable?" He rubbed her stomach.

Kelsi tensed. "I probably should get up and stretch." She smiled. "Maybe the other exhibits are more encouraging."

He squeezed her hand. "I wouldn't count on it, judging from this one." Stephan stood and helped her to her feet. They strolled back into the grand foyer. Across the hall, an exhibit was still packed with people spilling into the hall and that's where she spied a buffed guy with rich dark skin, holding court with Lindsay. Her sister seemed to be captivated by him. *Interesting.*

The backdrop in the room was a majestic pageantry of what appeared to be an African king and queen on a throne. She peeped through the crowd for Tyler and her parents, but they were nowhere in sight. Neither was Raimond. So much for wanting reconciliation. *He invites me, then ignores me.* Kelsi's feelings shouldn't be hurt, but they were. She twisted her lips in disappointment.

A childish part of her wanted him to beg for her forgiveness. She wanted him to be miserable like she felt as a lost little girl who couldn't understand why her daddy didn't love her anymore. She sighed. Those emotions were very petty, but so real.

All thoughts of Raimond were dismissed when Kelsi spied a corner buffet loaded with fruits and desserts. As she was about to point Stephan in that direction, someone called her name. She and Stephan turned at the same time. To Kelsi's surprise, Eva was walking her way.

"Eva!" Kelsi met her halfway. As they hugged, Kelsi tried to absorb some of her friend's cheerfulness. When Kelsi released Eva and stepped back, the two admired each other.

"It looks like we wear blue well." Eva grinned.

"I agree." Kelsi giggled too.

Stephan cleared his throat.

"Oh." Kelsi wrapped her arm around his. "I'm sorry, Eva, this is my husband and the father-to-be, Stephan."

"Hello." She shook hands with Stephan.

"It's nice to put a name to a face. My wife has mentioned you."

"I was about to send my hubby for food over there," Kelsi said, then looked at Stephan. "Hon, do you mind getting two plates?"

Eva waved her hand. "I can get Kidd—"

"I don't mind," Stephan said and took off to do their bidding.

Kelsi faced Eva again, and they both spoke at the same time. "What are you doing here?" They laughed.

Suddenly, Kelsi was distracted in her peripheral view of Raimond laughing with a small group. Evidently, he hadn't given her presence a second thought. She blinked and it seemed like his countenance changed. Before her eyes, a wounded expression plagued him every time he eyed a woman not far away. And she thought his pitiful look was reserved for her.

Raimond hadn't changed as he said—liar. Either the pretty lady was purposely ignoring him or she was unaware of his interest. *Run, honey, he will break your heart.* She composed her emotions and answered Eva who seemed to be waiting for a reply. "I just asked myself the same question. I shouldn't have come."

"What do you mean?" Eva frowned.

"The man who opened this place is my missing-in-action biological father. He's a jerk and two-timer. He hounded me as if he wanted to reconcile—*please give me another chance, I want to make it up to you...yada yada yada*, but all he's done is eye—no, lust—over that woman over there. I don't care what he says, he's probably sleeping with her."

Eva squinted in the direction Kelsi pointed. "Your father—" she stuttered.

Kelsi cut her off. "He is not my father."

"Okay, sorry." She nodded. "Raimond Mayfield is definitely not sleeping with that woman."

"How do you know?" Kelsi frowned. "Do you know her?"

"Yes. That's Sandra, my mother-in-law."

Kelsi's stomach seemed to sink as her knees became weak under the pressure of her embarrassment. She quickly mustered up an apology. "I'm sorry. Your mother-in-law seemed so perfect."

"She is as perfect as God sees her. He broke it off with her to focus on mending his relationship with you."

"Eva, I hope you won't think badly about me, but I don't

know the man and that tidbit doesn't make me feel any differently toward him. When I look at him, all I see is desertion, rejection, and a woman chaser. I don't want a relationship with him, so I don't even know why I came." Kelsi gnawed on her lips. Maybe it was her hormones.

"I'll be right back." Eva marched away.

Was she going to get Sandra and force Kelsi to apologize to her too? The day was going from bad to worse. As she scanned the museum for Stephan, Kelsi couldn't help being impressed with Raimond's endeavor.

She saw Eva was heading her way again, this time with a muscular-build man that kept her close as if he was her bodyguard. Where Eva could be described as pretty and dainty, the man with her was dark and had a ruggedness to him that was sexy. Kennedy favored the man. He had to be Eva's husband.

Eva, Kidd, and Stephan made it to Kelsi at the same time. "You two need to talk," Eva said by way of introductions.

"Huh?" Stephan looked as confused as Kelsi when Eva relieved Stephan of one of the plates and handed it to Kelsi, then steered Stephan away, chatting as if they were old friends.

"Do you know what's going on?" Kelsi asked Eva's husband.

"Unfortunately, I do," Kidd said. "Let's find you a seat first."

As he led her to a sectional for privacy, she glanced over her shoulder at Stephan who had the same confusion in his eyes.

Chapter

Sixteen

Kidd wasn't looking forward to *this* talk. Actually, it would be another discussion that centered on Raimond. The previous night, his mother had invited him over and they talked, really talked, about Samuel and Raimond. They both had cried as they unburdened their souls, although he would never admit that he *boo-hoo*ed in his mother's arms, not even to Ace or Eva.

Now it appeared he was about to have another heart-to-heart talk. From the bewildered appearance on Kelsi's face to the determined one set on Eva's as she devoured whatever was on that plate in her hand to the suspicious glare from Kelsi's husband, Kidd wondered why he was put on the hot seat.

His wife was bossy, but he knew how to set boundaries, which of course, Eva crossed whenever she felt he was being unreasonable. He looked at Kelsi again who seemed just as uncomfortable as him. "Congratulations on your baby. My wife says the baby is your first one."

Kelsi nodded, then turned her attention on the pieces of fruit screwed on a long stick like a shish kebab. "Ah, I'm sorry for what I said about your mother..."

"Excuse me?" Kidd's body tensed. Eva didn't relay that part. "Exactly *what* did you say about *my* mother?"

"Nothing worth repeating." She offered a weak smile, which made Kidd more suspicious. "I didn't know Sandra was your mother."

That's not important. I have drawn your wretched soul with loving kindness, God scolded him.

Kidd swallowed and submitted to whatever the Lord was chastening him for. "Apology accepted. My wife thought we should talk because we both have something in common."

"Oh? What could that be?" She sipped on juice, seemingly clueless.

Kidd studied his hands, exhaled, then answered, "We both have issues with our fathers for abandoning us—"

"Actually," she interrupted and jutted her chin in the air and squared her shoulders. "Raimond did me a favor. Because of his infidelity, I got an upgrade for a dad."

"You had more than me," Kidd said softly. "There was no low-grade, upgrade, or stand-in for a father. I knew she sacrificed a lot for my brother and me, but I didn't realize really how much until recently. I was a boy, trying to be the man, her protector..." He bowed his head. "And I'll admit, I carried that burden and responsibility with me all through life and even now, it's hard to relinquish that role in her life."

He didn't expect her to understand. It was the oldest man-child's weight in a single parent household. His mind drifted to the countless times he caused his mother heartache with his "man of the house" attitude when it came to her and Ace.

The music jolted him back to the present. He didn't enjoy returning to Memory Lane twice in a week. "And for the record, I'm not fond of Raimond either, so that's two things we have in common, but you have something I will never have."

Kelsi raised an eyebrow. "Which is?"

"A chance for closure." Kidd could no longer say that Sandra Nicholson had an affair with a man who she didn't know was married at the time, but still in his protective mode, he would never repeat that nugget, not even to Ace, if he hadn't heard it with his own ears. He cleared his throat and chose his words carefully. "My parents never married—" he was about to add "don't judge" but that always came off as saying, "I already know it's wrong and who are you to remind me?" "—But my brother and I are a product of their love. I lived with pure hatred for the man and wanted the first opportunity to throw the first punch, then we learned that he had died and I thought all the fight within me died too. But I'm still angry and it doesn't seem like I can get rid of it."

Come unto Me and I'll give you rest, God whispered Matthew 11:25.

Kidd chuckled to himself. Jesus had been saying that to him for years, but after the big fallout, Kidd was beginning to understand that the choice to hold on to the burden or give it to the Lord was up to him.

Kelsi sucked on a strawberry, reminding Kidd that Kennedy did the same thing. He hadn't meant to reveal so many raw emotions to Kelsi, who was in essence, a stranger, but his wife assigned him to this mission and he was going to see it to the end for whatever it was worth. "When I met your father who was wooing my mother, all I saw was Samuel

Jamieson. My protective instincts kicked in and I was gearing up for a showdown." He released a dry chuckle. "But to Raimond's credit, he held his own and reasoned with me that people change. Maybe if Samuel was alive, he could be saved today, or not."

He shrugged. "More than anything I wish I had that closure by confronting him, and I'm praying one day that I will stop taking things off the cross that Christ put on there." Kidd glanced up and saw Raimond freeze in his tracks when he noticed Kidd talking to his daughter. The uncertainty on the man's face put Kidd in a mischievous mood. Let the man think that Kidd was stirring the pot. He turned back to Kelsi without giving Raimond any clue of what was being discussed. "The bitterness was eating me alive like cancer. Take the chance, Kelsi. Talk to him. It will help you move on."

"I have moved on," she insisted verbally, but her eyes held an untold story.

Kidd grunted. "I don't know you well enough to call you a liar." She flinched. "But I've said those very words countless times and I was lying to myself. If not today, or tomorrow, take the chance and get your closure. Raimond may not say what you want to hear, but the truth will certainly make you free. Now, I've said my piece." He was about to stand, but Kelsi stopped him as she dabbed her mouth. Kidd didn't hide his shock when he glanced at her now empty plate that seemed minutes earlier had enough fruit and cheese on it for two people.

"Thank you for saying that," she said softly. "Parents don't seem to understand that we, the children—" she patted her chest, "—are devastated at the loss of a mom or dad, whether it's in death or neglect. We want our *mommy* and *daddy,* as is, off the sale floor—we don't care about grownup stuff."

Kidd smirked and raised his hand and she did the same for a high five. They did have a kindred spirit, because that was exactly how he felt when Samuel's visits became less frequent.

Kelsi's eyes watered. "If they abandon the other person because of unresolved issues, children can't process separation and divorce."

"I hear you," Kidd agreed. They both were quiet as he got to his feet—one, because Eva was heading their way and two, because Kelsi's husband was almost there. "Raimond may not deserve you as a daughter, and I'm not sold on the idea that he's good enough for my mother either, but only time will tell."

Kidd prayed he gave Kelsi something to think about, so she wouldn't be tormented like he had been for years. Kidd also hoped that his mother's presence there would give Raimond second thoughts about losing a good woman. It wasn't easy to get his mother to come to the museum's grand opening, but his little Eva worked her charm. He didn't know what his wife had said or done, but Sandra Nicholson bounced back and was ready to take the world hostage. Kidd smiled. Maybe he was too old to play bodyguard to his mother and it was time to let another man take the job.

In either case, God had laid the groundwork through Kidd. It was up to Raimond how he would play the hand dealt.

Eva slipped an arm around him and brushed her lips against his. He wanted more, but their intimacy wasn't for public display. Pregnant or not, she would always be sexy to him.

"You okay, babe?" Stephan asked his wife, but kept an eye on him.

"Yes." She motioned to stand and Stephan guided her to her feet and kissed her as Eva had done him. "Honey, I think you and Kidd should get to know each other, because I would like us to remain friends."

What would Raimond say about them being friends? Kidd thought with a grin. Oh well, that was not his problem, because if Raimond didn't play his cards right, he wouldn't be in his mother's or daughter's lives anymore.

Chapter

Seventeen

When did Sandra get here? Raimond asked himself, remembering to breathe. The bigger question was why did she bother? Was she there to torture him with her beauty, but with a "don't come near me" snub when he was in arm's length?

Sandra moved throughout the place, seemingly content to evade him. She was unaware of the stares she was receiving, including his. She was a timeless beauty with the white garb draped over her ageless figure, giving her an angelic glow. When she did acknowledge him, it was in a cordial manner, nothing more.

Equally as beautiful was his baby girl who had blossomed into a stunning young woman. Kelsi was radiant as an expectant mother. He had lost the years in between that he could never get back. She looked like her mother when he and Ivy married. He hadn't expected her presence to paralyze him with fear of saying the wrong thing to send her running. He wanted to hug her and never let go, but Kelsi gave him a "don't even think about it" look.

So Raimond had backed off, giving her space to soften and hopefully to appreciate his work. While he entertained and networked with local businessmen, all Raimond could think about was getting to Kelsi. When he was able to break away and seek her out, he was shocked to see her huddled in a corner with, of all people, Kidd. Raimond could only imagine their plot of his demise. Not wanting to make a scene, Raimond had backed off and bided his time.

That's when he began to pray and he hadn't stopped. First, he gave thanks for the amazing turnout and offers for generous donations from prominent whites and blacks in the community. That kept the smile on his face, even as his heart ached.

Don't focus on what you don't have, but what I've given you, God whispered.

Of course, the Lord was right. He straightened his stance and took another glance at Sandra who was chatting away with the women in her family.

"Congratulations, man, you pulled it off," Townsend said, blocking his view. His friend had flown in from D.C., for this occasion. "Dace outdid himself with the sculptures, the music—" He whistled. "Top notch. Everything seems to have fallen in place."

Not everything, Raimond thought as he slipped his hands in his pockets and peeped over Townsend's shoulder and kept his eyes locked on his target. "Thanks."

"I thought you were going to need extra people for the exhibits, but somehow you've managed to find some engaging narrators for all of them."

"Huh?" Raimond had eight displays and only four people

had volunteered to give talks, which included Parke and his brother Cameron. The other displays were self-guided. "I don't."

Townsend chuckled. "Then you have been invaded." He pivoted on his heels and Raimond followed him.

He checked the biggest attraction: *The Journey* exhibit, which featured Dace's the African queen and her throne, the 3-D slave cemetery, and White House hologram. Even though it was meant to be a self-guided tour, Parke Jamieson mesmerized visitors with his historical knowledge and passion.

"We were kings and queen before we were captured and enslaved," Parke told the crowd as if he had some script memorized. "You see, my tenth great-grandfather, Paki Kokumuo Jaja, Chief Prince of the Diomande Tribe, was born in December 1770 in Cote d'Ivoire, Africa...

"His name means a 'witness that this one will not die.' But on that fateful day, he and his warriors were attacked, severely beaten, and kidnapped. Mande tribe leaders thought their country was too far westward and untouchable from slave traders, since they were nestled relatively safe between kingdoms that would later become French or British colonies, and eventually Liberia, Guinea, Mali, Burkina, and Ghana.

"In the sixteenth century, Amina was sixteen when she became queen of Zaria, Nigeria. Warriors had taught her military skills and she fought battles to protect her people during her thirty-four-year reign. Historians labeled her as 'a woman as capable as a man.' " He nodded at Raimond who gave him a mock salute to carry on and so Parke continued, "In 1821, freed enslaved people were boarded on ships leaving New Bedford, Massachusetts to be resettled in Liberia..."

"He knows his stuff," Townsend whispered. "We could use him at the Smithsonian."

Squeals, laughter, and applause drew Raimond and Townsend's attention. They strolled toward the excitement.

Worming his way through the spectators to the travel exhibit, featuring Stagecoach Mary, black cowboys and cowgirls, Raimond stopped in his tracks. Once again, Grandma BB was decked out in Stacy Adam shoes. This time, they were brownish marble. He hated to admit they did complement her stylish pantsuit. But what was she up to? Raimond hadn't assigned her to any program.

He frowned. He and Sandra had split before he could ask what the woman's real story was. Evidently, Sandra needed to take charge of the woman's shoe wardrobe.

"Mary Fields was my kin," Grandma BB boasted, weaving her tall tale.

"Do you think she's telling the truth?" Townsend gave him an odd look.

Raimond shrugged. "The woman wears men's shoes. How serious would you take her?"

As if Grandma BB could hear him breathing, she shot Raimond a snarl. "You see, I tote a gun just like my auntie. She was born enslaved in 1832, but she later became a stagecoach driver. I'm not six feet like she was, but, chile, let someone mess with me," she snapped and thumped her chest. "I kinda like the idea of a black woman in the Wild, Wild West carrying a pair of six-shooters." She struck a pose with her hands reaching for invisible holsters hanging off her waist. "Plus a ten-gauge shotgun. Cool, huh?" She shrugged as she paced the room. "Me personally, I like the .44 caliber colt."

Townsend covered his snicker with a cough. Raimond

couldn't contain his amusement and others chuckled too. If the woman had a rope, portraying DeBoraha Akin-Townson, the only African American female cowgirl to compete with a professional rodeo association card, she would probably hog-tie him as a demonstration.

"Don't count us senior citizens folks out," Grandma BB warned, "because Auntie Mary was my hero. She was sixty-two when she became a U.S. mail coach driver in Central Montana. She had a mule named Moses and I have an ex-police dog named Silent Killer…"

Raimond nudged Townsend. "Come on. That woman is mixing fact with fiction."

"We could use her in D.C. too," Townsend said underneath his breath as they strolled back into the foyer.

"Now, they are legit," Raimond stated, pointing to the Archway entrance where six theater major students were dressed in union uniforms as U.S. Color troops, reenacting reading of the Lincoln's proclamation, announcing all those enslaved for life were now free for life.

Whenever Raimond saw the reenactment, he thought about how Christ proclaimed he was free for life after He washed his sins away and gave Raimond spiritual power to keep him from falling.

In the local St. Louis history room, Parke's two younger brothers, Malcolm and Cameron, seemed to play tag team as they talked about Annie Malone, a chemist and first black female millionaire; the enslaved blacks on the Oregon Trail that began in St. Louis, highlighting Slave Robin Holmes who sued slave holders Nathaniel and Lucinda Ford for his children's freedom; and countless other stories that Raimond hadn't included.

"It looks like I have my own mini-Smithsonian staff," Raimond boasted with a grin. The Jamiesons, including the crazy lady, Grandma BB, were on his non-existent payroll. Then he sobered. "Hey, have you seen my daughter?" He really wanted to do whatever damage control after Kidd probably brainwashed her.

"She might have left," Townsend said softly. "I wish you would've let me talk to her about the new you." His friend shook his head.

Raimond's heart sank, but he managed a smile for Townsend's sake, then patted him on the shoulder. "Thanks, but she wouldn't have believed you."

"That's too bad."

"Yeah, well, maybe it's best that I didn't overwhelm her, but I'm glad she came" He grinned like the proud papa that he wanted to be. When he caught a glimpse of Sandra, standing alone, he excused himself.

"You're the most beautiful woman I've seen in a long time." He had kept track of the weeks.

"A person doesn't discard beautiful things," she stated without giving him a backwards glance. "They cherish them."

When she did face him, he pulled her into a trance, or was it the other way around? Beautiful was an understatement. Somehow, Sandra was prettier than before.

When her lips moved, Raimond realized Sandra was speaking.

"I commend you on your successful grand opening," Sandra said, then strutted away, leaving the sweet fragrance of perfume as her calling card.

Chapter

Eighteen

Sandra couldn't believe she did it. Against her better judgment she had let her daughters-in-law convince her to attend the museum's public grand opening and flaunt Raimond with her endowments God had preserved throughout the years. Did she have any regrets? Yes, because that had been out of her character to deliberately try to get a man's attention for personal satisfaction. Did it work? She doubted it, because it had been a week and she hadn't heard from Raimond Mayfield.

"Mom, you know I love you as a mother, friend, sister, much more than a mother-in-law," Talise began softly as Sandra sat in the chair at Talise's small salon she and Ace owned.

Working a couple of days a week, Talise had built up a clientele. Thanks to happy customers and family referrals, she only needed to work part-time hours as a Southwest Airlines ticket agent to keep her perks for the family to fly at a discount. Plus, it gave her more time to enjoy being mommy to Lauren.

"I know." Sandra smiled as she shut down all thoughts of her ex beau. Talise's endearment meant something was on her daughter-in-law's mind with an intro like that.

Shutting off the hand dryer, Talise spun the chair around for Sandra to face her. She finger-brushed Sandra's hair out of her eyes as if to have full view. "You were honest with me when Ace and I split up. I trusted you as a friend, although I knew it wasn't easy for you to see me date and move on with my life after your son rejected me."

Yes, that had been hard, but God was in control and ordered her steps, Sandra thought.

"Well, it's my turn to be on the sidelines and root for your happiness, which is why I'm on team Raimond."

"What?" Sandra blinked as Talise spun her back around and resumed her task as if she hadn't stated something earth-shattering. Raimond had a fan club among the Jamiesons after he broke her heart? Even he might be surprised.

"Hmm-um. There's no way you would have me go through the trouble of styling your updo and experimenting with new makeup for the grand opening, if deep down in your heart you were dead-set against it. I imagined he drooled, which was your intent. I heard you gush about the things you two did after every outing. I saw the chemistry between you two at Grandma BB's party and I saw the light dim from your eyes the following day when you said it was over. I know love when I see it." She bent and kissed Sandra's cheek and grinned. "I married your son, didn't I?"

"Yes, you did." Sandra's eyes misted as she smiled. She fumbled with her fingers as Talise tilted her head down. "I know that was petty of me to try a stunt like that when his focus was on the success of his museum."

Sandra had been impressed with the turnout. Whoever did his PR should be commended. There was the write-up in the *St. Louis American* newspaper, listing Raimond's background with the Smithsonian, even a couple of radio stations mentioned The Heritage House's grand opening as a not-to-be-missed event.

Despite being bombarded with media reminders of Raimond, Sandra was determined not to go and get a report from Parke, Malcolm, and Cameron, who were excited to be a part of the celebration about black history.

The Jamiesons were known to turn any cultural event into a celebration of that heritage and Sandra oftentimes mingled with the family, but not this time.

Raimond's rejection, even though he called it a time-out, stung. It was as if he reeled her into a web of happiness, then released her like a yo-yo.

Of course, the Jamieson wives didn't agree with her decision. *Cheney, Parke's wife, had been the ringleader. The woman was Talise's cousin-in-law. And usually where Cheney was, Grandma BB was close by. The pair had a history as neighbors and on outward appearances, the two didn't get along, but it was a ploy. Grandma BB was a lion and Cheney and her family were like her cubs.*

"It's a public event and if it wasn't for it being sponsored by Raimond, you would go anyway," Cheney tried to reason with her.

Grandma BB twisted her lips. "You're grown, chile. I never let a man stop me from going anywhere, anytime, with anybody, for anything... I have my army of senior citizens and tactically trained for..."

Cheney had rolled her eyes and tsked. "We know you're out of control." She frowned at the elderly woman who was also her former neighbor. "God provides the backup, no weapons or a contingency of red hats ladies necessary."

The other Jamieson wives: Hallison, Eva, and Gabrielle had also chimed in. Before long, Sandra had the confidence that she was big, bad, and grown as Grandma BB had boasted. But it was Eva's sermonette that sealed the deal, per se.

"Sandra, Jesus purchased you with the ultimate sacrifice that you belong to Him first. And I'm sure somewhere in Ephesians 3 says, 'Unto him that is able to do exceeding abundantly above all that we ask or think, according to the power that worketh in us.' That same God can give you a man who exceeds your expectations. So go, girl, and get whatever man God has for you out there!"

Eva had received the high fives from the other women in the room. Sandra had been the last one to lift her hand, and she knew she couldn't go back now. Plus, she wanted to see if Raimond had taken her suggestion about blacks' contributions in fashion.

Sandra might as well have been Cinderella with all the fuss the Jamieson women were making over her. Talise had been amused as she tagged along with Sandra when she shopped for the perfect attire, gently teasing her as if Sandra was going to her first prom, because she wanted to create the perfect image.

If Kidd was surprised that she was attending, he kept his thoughts to himself. At least she would have Kidd and Eva with her in case she wanted to make a fast getaway, since Talise and Ace had a previous engagement.

So with a fake calm, Sandra had stepped into The

Heritage House Museum as if she was one of the main attractions. Of course, seeing clients and others she knew helped ease the tension.

She strolled through one exhibit after another captivated, but when she eyed Raimond's black fashion exhibit, Sandra was wowed. The man showed off. Then again, Raimond had worked at the Smithsonian where Lois K. Alexander-Lane's black fashions collection was on display. It boasted more than seven hundred garments from a preserved slave dress to a ball gown, along with hundreds of accessories. She hadn't even mentioned the women's collection after she set out to prove a college instructor wrong about blacks' contribution in the fashion industry.

Of course, Raimond's display wasn't that extensive, but it was noteworthy. Sandra envisioned ensembles in 3-D, giving attention to how a client looked from the front, back, and side—the complete package. And that's what she would have brought to this showcase, a life-like mock store window on a platform, highlighting decades of fashions either designed by blacks or worn by black models.

Sandra moaned her delight when Talise massaged oil into her scalp, pulling her out of her reverie. Thanks to her daughter-in-law, her hair was healthy, thick, and always garnered compliments from Raimond.

She sighed. Her thoughts always found their way back to Raimond. At the museum, he had turned the tables on her instead of the other way around. Raimond had been the tease as her heart fluttered whenever he was near as if he was subconsciously on her radar. That day Sandra accepted what her heart had known since their first kiss. She had taken a chance on love, given in to Raimond's chase, and been captured. If there was another man out there for her, he had a tough act to follow, because Raimond Mayfield had been the real deal.

When Talise began to flat-iron Sandra's hair, she chatted away as if she knew what was on her mind. "He's the one I would pick for you and not because he's good-looking and successful and dotes on you, but he makes you smile."

Sandra smiled. "True, but I need to be some man's priority. I get that he's trying to make up for lost time with his daughter, but as an adult, she has her own life. Parents take a backseat to that life when children begin their families, or at least, I've tried to stay out of the way when my sons married wonderful women."

Talise leaned down and smacked a hard kiss on her cheek. Sandra felt loved, but not by the man she wanted—again. She sighed. "I saw his daughter from afar—beautiful and glowing like Eva, but she also has the potential of dangling a carrot over Raimond as a guilt trip to make him earn points to cash in to be in her good graces. That may take a lifetime, so he doesn't have time for me."

"I disagree. He wants what you already have."

"And what could that possibly be?" Sandra chanced a glance at her reflection in the mirror to see Talise's process.

"You have always had your sons. Raimond hasn't. You have reared them, watched them mature." Talise paused, possibly recalling a time when her husband's lack of maturity was to blame for them breaking up. "You've witnessed every special moment in their lives: jobs, marriage, babies... Raimond has none of that in his memory bank. Maybe, he needs a little hand-holding as he finds his way to create memories."

Hand-holding. Sandra missed those little things they shared, including him watching her when she least expected. It was as if he was cataloging everything about her. Then there was their embrace that seemed to connect their hearts. "So you think I'm not being sympathetic to his situation? He broke it off, not me, with demands. I didn't put enough value on my heart a long time ago. I love him, Talise, but I'm not the same woman I was when I fell in love with Samuel. I'm stronger, wiser, and definitely, not desperate."

Talise rested the flat iron on her counter and began to comb through Sandra's curls.

"Great speech, Mom, but I can hear it in your voice that your heart is bleeding. And I believe that's because he's lost without you too."

Sandra shook her head and it wasn't to test the body of her curls. "I don't think so, sweetie. I went there as a reminder of what he had, which included me strolling away on shaky legs. I might have caused my hips to sway a little more than usual."

Talise giggled. "Go, Momma Nicholson."

Sandra's shoulder dropped. "Yeah, but my dignity was tested as I willed myself not to cry." She swallowed, then whispered, "I didn't know that dating at my age could hurt so much as it had when I was twenty-one."

What crushed her was Raimond didn't try and stop her, so Sandra kept walking.

A few days later, a hot flash hit Sandra as she slowed to turn into the driveway of her condo. It wasn't the norm for her to come home and find an irresistible fine black man, braving the heat, sitting on her porch with flowers in one hand…and a bag of dog food in another? What was Raimond doing here?

It had to be a mirage or maybe she was experiencing a flashback from some thirty years earlier in New York City. Samuel Jamieson had been waiting for her as she returned from an interview where she had secured a coveted internship at Saks Fifth Avenue.

She and Samuel had met the night before when he used his jacket as a canopy to shield her from a downpour on her way back to her hotel. She mentioned she was in town for the interview and there he was sitting on the bench outside the hotel with a single rose. That unexpected gesture stole her heart and it took years—no, most of her life—for her to get it back. Of course, if Samuel had been an honorable married man that scenario would have never happened and neither would her sons.

The past faded and the future came into view when Raimond stood. Unlike Samuel, Raimond had been honest with her from the start and Sandra was aware of his past discretions and current distraction—Kelsi. So why was he here instead of working to get in Kelsi's good graces? Was the dog food for him to eat crow, or for Boston?

Sandra slid out of her car and watched as Raimond strode within feet of her and stopped, staring. When a short-lived breeze stirred, Sandra inhaled a hint of his cologne mixed with his perspiration. The intensity in Raimond's eyes made Sandra shiver.

When his nostrils flared, Sandra hoped there were remnants of her perfume to drug her as his had done her.

Besides holding the bag of pet food, he wore a puppy dog expression that melted her heart. Talise's words that he was lost without her reverberated in his defense revolved in her head, but Sandra refused to succumb to Raimond's good looks—his goatee had a few more slivers of silver, but still sculptured the outline of his lips and the peach polo shirt and ceased khakis did more than show off his biceps, but a trimmed waist. She had to resist his charm and fight for her self-worth. "Raimond," she said softly, "why are you here?"

Swallowing hard, Raimond looked uncertain. "How many reasons do I need for you to invite me in? It's hot outside and I could use a tall glass of iced tea."

Sandra tried to keep a straight face, but gave up and laughed at his pitiful state. "Come on." She walked past him. "I've got a pitcher of iced tea you can take with you."

"I was hoping you would enjoy a glass with me," he mumbled, but Sandra didn't respond.

Once they were inside her condo, Sandra released Boston from his kennel. Instead of making the detour to go outside, he raced to Raimond as if he could read the words on the package.

Raimond squatted and rubbed the dog's head then stood and stuffed his hands in his pockets. "I've been praying."

"A good thing," she said, then grabbed Boston's leash to take him for a quick walk.

"I can do that," he offered and she didn't argue as she put her pet in his care. "For you." He handed her the small bouquet.

They were the same flowers he had given her on their first date. "Thank you," she choked out and performed a series of inhales and exhales to calm her pounding heart. He remembered. Sandra's resolve slipped.

Minutes later, she watched out the window as Boston led

Raimond to the island most neighbors called the puppy yard.

Lord, why is he here? Sandra gnawed on her lips in the interim, filling a vase with water, then arranging the flowers. *What had God been telling Raimond that He hadn't shared with her?* she wondered.

God hadn't answered her by the time man and beast returned. Sandra had a tall glass of iced tea waiting for Raimond and cool water for Boston.

Raimond gulped down the glass, then reached for the pitcher and poured more. Sandra folded her arms and leaned against the counter, ticking off the seconds for an answer. He set the empty glass down. "I'm here about us."

"There is no us. That I do remember. You made that clear." She sidestepped him to the refrigerator to slide the pitcher on the shelf. When Sandra turned around, Raimond was rooted in place.

He seemed precise in his movements. Pulling her into a trance, he quietly approached like a lion cornering his prey until he towered over her. "Baby—"

She blinked and arched an eyebrow at the endearment.

"What I mean is you've had years to reconcile and right the wrongs of your past."

How can a woman right the wrong of sleeping with another woman's husband? she wanted to say, but didn't like the sound of it.

"God has me on this journey. I can't do this without you. I've tried, but I can't."

Don't fall for it, Sandra coaxed herself. "What are you saying?"

Raimond reached behind him and pulled something colorful out of his back pocket, then dangled it before her eyes.

"You need me to tie your tie?"

When she tried to push him away, he gently restrained her wrists and pulled her closer.

He lowered his voice to that Barry White husky quality. "You can strangle me first for being an idiot and not cherishing the gift God had given me. After you resuscitate me, I want us to start over."

"And I'm supposed to just forgive you for hurting me?" Her eyes misted.

Shaking his head, Raimond whispered, "No. You're supposed to put the man who loves you in the doghouse and let him earn his way back into your heart. I went about trying to win back Kelsi's love the wrong way. In the end, the choice is hers. Now, I'm desperate to win you back, please, Sandra."

"So you love me?" She had to hear it one more time.

"More each day, whether we're together or apart."

She wanted to do a Whitney Houston jump like the singer had done into Bobby Brown's arms, but that wasn't her style. So she took a deep breath and debated on how she should respond.

Sandra didn't hide her amusement as she requested his silk tie. "Hand it over."

He swallowed. "Are you going to strangle me?"

"No," she whispered, stroking his cheek. Then she wrapped the tie around his neck and under the polo shirt's collar. "How about an Eldredge knot?"

As she concentrated, Sandra noted Raimond's breathing was uneven until he leaned forward. Her heart pounded as she waited for their lips to touch.

The tie was easily forgotten and so was the past as Raimond wrapped his arms around her waist and Sandra collapsed against his chest.

Chapter

Nineteen

Kelsi wasn't moved by her sister's tantrum. She had made up her mind the day she saw Sandra at the museum to bow out of the tea party.

"What do you mean you're not going after you dragged me from one store to another looking at hats, pearls, and gloves?" Lindsay's scowl made it clear that she wasn't having it. "We're going, sister, even if you go into labor."

Instead of suffering in the July heat and humidity, she and Lindsay decided to stay in and watch movies, play board games, or do nothing. Evidently, Kelsi had killed the mood when she shared the news. Plus, Lindsay hadn't handed over the pint of ice cream Kelsi had requested.

"You're not supposed to bully a pregnant woman." Kelsi waved her hands frantically for Lindsay to give her the bag. "Besides, that was before my 'day at the museum.'" She wrote imaginary quote marks with her fingers, feeling like actor Ben Stiller in the old movie *Night at the Museum* where everything seemed to go wrong.

"Before what?" Lindsay pressed, not relinquishing her possession of Kelsi's treat.

Kelsi sighed as she lounged in the baby's nursery. For the last two weeks, she had kept her thoughts to herself, not even sharing with Stephan how the visit to the museum had shook her up. "By the time I left, I felt like I had three strikes against me."

"Hold that thought. This sounds serious." Lindsay hurried out the room, rummaged through the utensils drawer in the kitchen, then returned with bowls and spoons. "Sounds like both of us are going to need this ice cream."

Rubbing her stomach, Kelsi pushed back in the rocker. That museum visit did seem like a mental nightmare by the time she left. Stephan contributed to her exhaustion, but Kelsi knew it was disappointment.

"Okay." Lindsay scooped up helpings for them and handed Kelsi her share. They clicked the bowls as a toast, mumbled a blessing over the treat, and dug in.

Once Lindsay was situated on a large square ottoman, mimicking a building block with an alphabet letter on each side, she gave Kelsi her full attention. "Was it from the shock of seeing Raimond, who by the way, looks great for his age." She grinned. "I didn't say anything at the time, but you have his eyes."

"Whatever." Kelsi rolled those eyes. "Raimond was only part of the problem. What was I thinking about going to his shindig as if I supported all his endeavors?" She slipped another spoonful of ice cream in her mouth and barely let it melt before continuing, "If I hadn't gone, then I would never have learned that my almost next best friend's fantastic mother-in-law, Sandra, is my estranged biological father's love interest. How can I accept Eva's invitation now? It would be awkward."

"Did Sandra say anything to you or look at you oddly?" Lindsay asked in a cautious tone as if she was one step away from retaliating.

"No. Kidd said Raimond broke it off with her to devote all his time on rebuilding our relationship." Licking the spoon, Kelsi shook her head. "From where I was sitting, Raimond only had eyes for Sandra, but she ignored him."

Lindsay ate her share of the ice cream with gusto. As she scrapped the bottom of the bowl, she mumbled, "Bummer. I really wanted to go. It sounded like so much fun. I'm surprised we never had any tea parties with Momma. I Googled tea parties—to make sure we were in full costume—" she quickly added. "Did you know there were African American Tea rooms?"

"No." Kelsi shook her head. Her interest was rekindled.

"They were a big deal and catered to elite and upper middle class blacks. Notable groups such as the NAACP Women's Auxiliary and the Negro Business League booked tea rooms for luncheons and dinners."

"Interesting." Kelsi added that morsel of history to the other bits and pieces of African American facts she had picked up at the museum. "So I guess Sandra is keeping the tradition going."

Secretly, Kelsi was disappointed of backing out too. She was excited about learning more of how it was done, so she could pass it down to the daughter she planned to have after Baby Stephan, but how could she go and not feel uncomfortable? "That's amazing."

"Yep, and listen to this. Mattel even sold African

American Barbie Tea Time play sets in the late 1990s. Plus, there was a big uproar in the White House when First Lady Lou Hoover invited Jessie DePriest, a black woman and wife of a black Illinois congressman, to have tea with her. Girl, a scandal ensured. Mrs. Hoover received letters complaining that the White House was for white people, and not Negroes, and she should have more pride than to put herself on the same level with niggers."

"What!" Kelsi's jaw dropped, then she closed it. "Good for Mrs. Hoover."

Lindsay stood and gave Kelsi a high five. "That was in 1929 and I guess haters have the same resentment today with President Obama and First Lady Michelle Obama in the White House."

"Racism will not die," Kelsi said then remembered what was said after the films clips she and Stephan watched at the museum about praying for haters. Someone would have to pray for her before she could pray for those losers. Rubbing her stomach, Kelsi glanced around the cheerful nursery, then stared at nothing. "I don't want to bring my baby into a world with so much hate."

"Hey," Lindsay called her out of her musing. "What's going on in your head?"

"Well, after one heartbreaking exhibit, it seemed odd for the presenter to say, 'Mr. Mayfield wants blacks to pity them for their atrocities against our ancestors, because they don't know Jesus, and we need to show Christian love at all costs where our reward comes from God,' or something like that." Kelsi braced herself as Baby Stephan stole the show and stretched. She and Lindsay watched with fascination, then laughed.

Once the baby stilled, Kelsi twisted her lips in thought. "I went to the grand opening expecting Raimond to beg for my forgiveness and me to gloat, but for some reason he kept his distance and that annoyed me."

Lindsay *tsk*ed and didn't hide her disappointment. "That was evil."

"Yeah, I know." She paused. "He's called since then, and I'm back to not wanting to talk to him again and he still leaves messages and ends with, 'I pray that God will bless you and the baby.' " She frowned. "It's strange."

"Awww. Well…" Lindsay stood and grabbed Kelsi's bowl. "I say since your issue is with Raimond and not Sandra, accept the tea party invitation. Don't tell me you're not curious."

"Okay, okay." Kelsi laughed and rolled her eyes. "Maybe a little."

"Yay." Lindsay danced in place and grinned. "The party starts at two, I'll pick you up at one-fifteen. I definitely don't want to be late."

Once she disappeared down the hall toward the kitchen, Kelsi closed her eyes. Her sister's happiness might be short-lived, and if Sandra gave off any negative vibes, then they both were out of there.

The next afternoon, Lindsay showed up at Kelsi's dressed from head to toe in vintage clothing. No wonder her sister was determined to go.

"Wow, can we say rolling '30s?" Kelsi chuckled.

Lindsay waved her hand and strutted inside, then spun around as if she was a model. She eyed Kelsi's attire and shook her head. "And can we say you didn't get the memo?"

"I'm very pregnant, if you haven't noticed." She pointed

her lace-gloved hands to her stomach. The fabric was itched and the pearl necklace seemed like it was choking her. But she did sport a fashionable floppy hat.

"Not to worry. I found some extra things to enhance your beauty." Lindsay batted her eyes at the same time Stephan walked into the foyer.

"Impossible." Stephan kissed Lindsay's cheek, then chuckled at her getup.

"Men." She shooed Stephan off and grabbed Kelsi's hand. "Come, we don't have much time." She lifted her bag of goodies.

As an unwilling participant, Kelsi watched as her sister switched out her jewelry for a long string pearl necklace. Lindsay added large pearl drop earrings and tossed aside the lace gloves for long white cloth ones, which were more comfortable.

Kelsi nodded and admired her reflection in the mirror. "Great. Let's go."

"One minute." Lindsay dug in her bag and whipped out a large straw hat that was airy and decorated with pearls.

"Wow." She squinted. "Did you, Eva, and her mother-in-law go shopping together?"

"No, silly. I didn't know secondhand stores had such treasures." Lindsay angled the headpiece on Kelsi's head and helped her out of the chair. "Now, kiss your husband goodbye and let's go."

Soon they were headed to the address that Eva supplied. It had been a while since Kelsi dressed up. She felt more like she was dolled up for somebody's church than an outing. *Church.* She and Stephan would have to pick one once the baby came, so they could be good Christian parents, not that she and Stephan were bad people. Church was simply a ritual people performed on Sundays. Her family and Stephan's routine had always been other engagements and obligations. Church got pushed out of the way in the scuffle.

When Lindsay pulled up into the gated community, fear struck Kelsi and her baby must have sensed it too, because he started moving wildly. *Was this an omen?* she wondered, taking steady breaths. Would she be welcomed? Would Sandra be bitter that Raimond dumped her? Would the woman feel obligated because Eva invited her? The questions abounded as Lindsay found the house number and parked.

Kelsi swallowed and took more deep breaths as Lindsay turned off the ignition. "Hey, everything is going to be all right. If there are any signs of trouble, Stephan has this location in his GPS and will drop everything to rescue his wife."

"I know." Kelsi smiled and got out after a few false starts to move her body. Taking a look around, Kelsi noted the landscape. It was serene with a fountain, walking trail, and bungalows mixed with apartments.

Lindsay adjusted her hat, then tended to Kelsi's. With their arms looped together, she and Lindsay began what they used to call as children, the "Yellow Brick Road" synchronized stroll to the doorway. They could hear the laughs from the other side of the door before Lindsay knocked.

Kelsi blinked at the woman who opened the door. She could only be described as regal with her bloody red lipstick, earrings, pearls, and hat that swallowed most of her head.

"Hello, darling," she said and took a long drag on an imaginary cigarette that should have been in the holder hanging between her fingers. To Kelsi's relief, the woman wasn't smoking, giving her another reason for her to go back home, so as not to endanger her son. She glanced at the woman's feet and blinked. How did men's shoes go along with the tea party theme?

Her mind screamed, *Houston, we have a problem.*

But it was Eva who screamed her delight as she hurried to hug her first, then Lindsay, after gushing about her attire.

When Kelsi scanned the room for Sandra, she was glad Lindsay had upgraded her wardrobe, because these women were serious dressers for their afternoon tea.

"Let me make the introductions." Eva waved the guests over to her. "You met Grandma BB at the door." The elderly woman curtsied and a bone cracked. Everyone crackled, even Kelsi and Lindsay. "Next is the hostess, my mother-in-law, Sandra."

Sandra gave her a warm smile and hug, despite Kelsi's stiffening. "We can chat later if you like," she whispered.

"This is Talise, my sister-in-law and family hair stylist in residency. The rest are my cousins-in-law, Cheney, Hallison or Hali, and Gabrielle."

They gave a singsong hello. "Finally, the little ladies— under the watchful eye of their big cousin, Kami, is my daughter." She pointed to a kiddie table where three girls were about to sit. They wore rhinestone tiaras instead of hats. "Kennedy, remember the lady from the doctor's office? Can you say hi?"

When Kennedy shook her head and hid behind Kami's legs, everyone laughed. "And the other one is my niece and daughter's sidekick, Lauren. Put those together and it's like all hands on deck."

Lindsay was the first to say, "Wow," at the intimate setup. Sandra's living room had been transformed into a tea room. There were three round tables draped with lace tablecloths and had vintage Tiffany lamps as centerpieces. There were mismatched china plate settings at each table. Kelsi did a mental head count to determine if she and Lindsay completed the guest invite.

Grandma BB made a major production as she rang a crystal bell.

"Ladies, please be seated," a deep voice commanded as a man appeared dressed in a butler's uniform. He introduced himself as Chip Dale. "Lindsay, you're welcome to sit at the pregnancy table. Chippanddale will serve us herbal tea," Sandra teased.

"That's okay," Lindsay answered quickly, shaking her head "You're not sticking me with two expecting women."

Everyone laughed and Grandma BB stood. "There's room at my and Sandra's table."

Her sister didn't seem to think twice as she took up the offer, and Kelsi didn't know how she felt about it as she and Eva got settled and Talise joined them. The miniature hat piled with fake flowers was tilted to the side and showcased the woman's healthy-looking hair. Her thick hair was the first thing Kelsi noticed. Kelsi could see why the woman was a stylist.

Kelsi leaned forward and whispered, "Why does our server go by two names?"

"Honey, he's a former strip-tease dancer," Grandma BB answered from the room. Whatever the woman's age, she had good hearing. "He still goes by Chip and I added the And Dale part."

Kelsi was speechless. At least the man had clothes on or Stephan would have a fit.

"Ooh. Put me on the guest list for the next tea," Lindsay said enthusiastically. Kelsi groaned with embarrassment. Eva's family was going to think the Coleman and Cole-Edwards women were out of control.

As Chippanddale served table to table, the conversation was lively and it ranged from fashions, courtesy of Sandra, who seemed genuinely delightful. Talise answered hair care questions, even Kelsi's. Then Grandma BB talked about her recent birthday party.

In addition to cookies and teacakes on the table, Chippanddale brought them healthy snacks of veggies and mini sandwiches.

Kelsi learned the food was courtesy of Grandma BB's coupon clippings, survey answering for gift cards, and secret shopper perks. There was enough food for thirty plus folks, not just their small group.

"Which one is Grandma BB's granddaughter?" Kelsi kept her voice low to no avail.

"All of them, chile." The woman nodded.

"You can't be in this family without her adopting you," Sandra added.

"Do you need one, Kel?" the woman said, shortening her name. "I run a rent a grandma franchise."

"Ah, that's okay," Kelsi stuttered and took a bite of her sandwich to keep from laughing while Lindsay held her stomach in tears, cracking up.

They played card games and Cheney led the discussion about the history of the African American tea rooms. Lindsay shared what she had learned in a crash course. Kelsi covered a belch as her baby pushed and stretched, then she felt something wet. "Uh-oh. Oh, no." She began to panic. "I think my water broke." Her eyes misted. "My baby's coming."

As pandemonium spread, Chippanddale looked the most stricken with fear as Kelsi glanced around the room for help. But all the mothers looked as scared as she felt.

Sandra and Lindsay were at her side immediately, trying to calm her as tears fell down her cheeks. "Call my husband! Call Stephan, Lindsay."

"I'll drive you." Lindsay's voice shook.

"No!" Kelsi gasped for air. "Stephan and I agreed. If he can't take me, then I should go by ambulance! We've waited too long for our baby for anything to go wrong."

"Unless the baby is coming now, you'll make it in time by car," Sandra said.

That wasn't what Kelsi wanted to hear. "Call an ambulance!" Kelsi insisted.

Sandra nodded for Talise to make the call. Squeezing her hand, Sandra's voice was soothing. "It's going to be okay. You're in a room full of praying women. Your son will be fine."

"How did you know I was having a boy?" A pain hit and Kelsi cried out.

"*Ssh*. Your father told me. He's happy for you." She smiled. "I'm not a threat to your relationship. I believe in a happy ending."

Kelsi wasn't feeling happy at the moment as she held her stomach. "What's taking so long?"

"Practice your breathing." Sandra rubbed her arm as she heard Eva frantically telling someone on the other end of the phone, "The baby is coming and we're heading to the hospital."

"Girl, you have a stubborn husband," Lindsay snapped. "Three times I had to tell him to meet us at St. Johns and not come here. Mom and Dad are on their way there too."

It took forever for the paramedics to arrive and assess her symptoms. "I'm having a baby! Can we just go?" Kelsi did her best not to scream.

All of a sudden, Grandma BB started freaking out and paramedics grew concerned about her. Kelsi moaned. This wasn't how she envisioned her baby coming into this world.

Cheney stopped praying and advised the medics, "She's fine. This always happens when we start to pray and wake up those demons in her."

"That ain't it!" Grandma BB snapped. "I don't mind being a grandma, but I don't want to see a baby born or I'll be scarred for life."

"Do you mind if I call Raimond?" Sandra asked hesitantly. "He knows you don't want him there, but I'm sure he would want to pray too."

Kelsi didn't answer as her son punched her gut, then she cried out in pain. Right now, she needed as much prayer as she could get, even if Grandma BB's devils wouldn't come out of her, whatever that meant. "Yes, call and ask him to pray for me and the baby." Kelsi swallowed. "He can meet the rest of the family at the hospital."

A tear slid down Sandra's cheek, and at the same time Kelsi felt one slide down hers.

Sandra kissed her cheek as they secured her on the stretcher. Lindsay held her hand and climbed into the back of the ambulance with her. Before another labor pain hit, Kelsi wondered what she had just done by allowing Raimond into her family circle.

Chapter

Twenty

"Raimond." Sandra spoke as calmly as she could from the passenger's seat in Talise's car while Grandma BB was stretched out in the back seat. They were dropping her off at her house after she refused medical attention. Maybe those were demons being exorcised from her. "Kelsi's water broke. The baby is coming."

When he didn't respond, Sandra asked, "Babe, are you okay?"

"Yeah," he choked out. "But she isn't due for another month or so."

Sandra smiled. Poor baby was out of practice on having a baby. "Evidently, that wasn't God's plan. She came to the tea party and we all prayed for her before the ambulance took her to St. Johns. She wants you to pray for her...and be there."

"What?" he shouted in her ear and Sandra giggled. "I advise you get to the hospital, Mr. Mayfield. You're about to become a grandpa."

He didn't even say goodbye as their call ended.

The short drive to the hospital in West County seemed twice as long. Once inside, the hospital staff directed them to the family waiting area. Kelsi and Stephan's families overpowered the room. Jamieson husbands were mingled in with them. Even Parke and Cheney's parents, Parke V and Charlotte, were on hand.

It was times like these she regretted not being a Jamieson, because they were truly one for all and all for one, even if Kelsi wasn't a Jamieson.

When Kidd noticed her, he greeted her with a kiss. Since their falling out and reconciliation, her son seemed to be more reserved. "Hey, Ma."

"Hey, son. What are you and the others doing here?"

"Eva called, said, 'having the baby' and 'on the way to St. Johns,' which is where she's delivering our baby." He rubbed the back of his neck. "I called everyone else, and you know them. Every Jamieson birth is another dot on the family tree. We didn't realize until we got here, it was the wrong baby about to be delivered."

"We'll laugh about it later, but right now, I'm trying to recover the years I lost at my house when Kelsi went into labor." Sandra chuckled. "You would think none of us have had babies, except Grandma BB, and that's another story." Glancing over Kidd's shoulder, Sandra glimpsed Raimond rushing in the room. He looked flustered, dazed, and nothing like the man who had stolen her heart. "Excuse me, son. I think Raimond needs me."

Kidd turned around and stared. Sandra had no idea what he was thinking, but she was glad when he consented, "He does, and I'm okay with that." He chuckled.

Raimond's usual neat appearance was sloppy with his shirt hanging outside his jeans. "Where is she?" He looked dazed. "Has the baby come?"

Sandra squeezed his hand and led him to an empty double seat. "No, sweetie. It may be a while. This is her first one."

Even in his vulnerable state, Sandra loved him and her feelings for him were rooted deep. She cared about him and everything and everyone close to him.

Closing his eyes, Raimond seemed to collapse in his seat. He was so quiet, Sandra thought he had dozed off, until his baritone voice drew her closer.

"Thank you for being there for Kelsi, praying, and calling me. I love you." He opened his eyes and looked at her.

"I know. I love you too."

Raimond hadn't moved from his seat, but that didn't stop others from coming over, mainly Jamiesons, and congratulating him.

"It seems strange to hear them say that. I only want to see my little girl."

"Kelsi's all grown up. She's going to be a mother herself," Sandra whispered and patted his hand. Their fingers had been intertwined since the moment he arrived. When Sandra tried to move away, his grip said otherwise.

"Ooh." Eva cringed across the room, holding her stomach.

Sandra shot her a warning look. "Don't you dare. I can't take two early arrivals in one day, especially since you have ten weeks to go."

Eva laughed, but her husband didn't look amused either. "Just teasing."

As the hours stretched, the children became restless and the elder Parke and Charlotte offered to take the grandchildren back to their house.

Soon the only ones remaining in the waiting room, besides Stephan and Kelsi's families, were Sandra with Raimond, Talise, and Eva. Eva refused to leave her friend. Talise refused to let her sister-in-law stay by herself—evidently, Sandra didn't count—and their husbands weren't going to let their wives out of their sights.

"Sweetie." Sandra nudged Raimond. "Do I have permission to go to the ladies' room?" she teased, which caused him to chuckle and relinquish his possession of her hand. Her daughters-in-law followed.

As they exited the ladies' room minutes later, Sandra pulled Eva aside. It was time for a mother-in-law's tough love. "I know you and Kelsi are becoming fast friends, but you're expecting too and you need to get your rest."

Eva nodded with a yawn. "Don't think my husband hasn't reminded me of that. One more hour and then I'll have Kevin take me home."

Sandra smiled and gave her a hug. "I'm glad you invited Kelsi and her sister, so that we could pray for her. My prayer is that God restores a relationship between father and daughter."

"Me too." Eva nodded.

"Like He has a certain couple." Talise grinned and reached for her hand before Sandra pulled her girls into a group hug.

"Forgiveness equals blessings," Sandra whispered.

When they returned to the waiting room, Raimond wasn't in his seat. Sandra thought perhaps he had taken a potty break when she noticed him across the room, speaking to both sets of the other expecting grandparents.

Sandra added that mending to her prayer list, so there

would be harmony among them for the baby's sake. Giving Raimond his space, Sandra returned to where they were sitting and closed her eyes.

She was startled from her rest when Stephan hurried into the room, yelling, "My son is here! He's here." His grin was wide, but his eyes and body seemed exhausted.

Immediately, everybody was on their feet and rushed to him with congratulations. As each set of parents went in, followed by siblings, Sandra prayed that Kelsi would extend mercy to Raimond.

Soon it was apparent that wasn't the case when Tyler and Lindsay appeared and didn't call for anyone else. Sandra's heart ached for Raimond as his shoulders slumped.

She rubbed his back, trying to soothe him as she had done his daughter, but she doubted it would have any effect if God didn't intervene, so she began to pray.

No good thing will I withhold from them who walk up rightly before me, God whispered Psalm 84:11.

Lord, I believe Raimond's a good man and is walking holy before You. Sandra's eyes misted. Only God knew Raimond's salvation report, so it was out of her hands.

Getting to his feet, Raimond squared his shoulders as if he was slipping back on his confidence, then Stephan came out the room.

"Raimond, would you like to see your grandson?"

A glow slowly spread across Raimond's face. *Thank You, God, for answering prayers.* Sandra was about to take her seat when Stephan added, "And you too, Sandra."

She blinked and patted her chest. Stephan nodded with a grin as he stepped back and waited for them to follow him. They washed their hands and donned sanitary protective clothing before proceeding to see the baby.

In the room, Kelsi was propped up in the bed, cuddling her newborn. Gone was the stylish hat and pearl lace, but the earrings still dangled from her lobes. She was glowing, but Sandra felt like an intruder as Kelsi stared at her father and Raimond stared at his first grandchild. Twice, Sandra had experienced that same awe that Raimond was probably experiencing for the first time. Yes, Talise had been right. Raimond did want what she already had and taken for granted.

Kelsi adjusted her baby as if he was alert to see his new visitors. "Stephan Evanston Raimond Edwards, meet your other grandpa." Her eyes brimmed with tears.

A tear fell from Raimond's eyes. His daughter had given him a happy ending.

Raimond found his voice as he moved closer to the bed. He bent and kissed Kelsi's cheek, something he had yearned to do for so long. And that contact sent warmth throughout his body. "I'm honored that you wanted your son to have a part of me."

"I'm a part of you, whether I accept you or not, but I do accept you." Her voice shook and she nodded. "And Sandra too. I may never understand why you did what you did when I was a little girl, nor your faith in God now, but I do know that I want to have a praying family like Sandra's for my son."

"'*And* we know that all things work together for good to them that love God, to them who are the called according to his purpose,' " Sandra whispered Romans 8:28 as Raimond reached for the sleeping boy and took a seat.

Sandra came forward and kissed Kelsi on the forehead and rubbed back her hair. "And you will have your praying family, because when God made a promise in the Books of Acts to all of us if we come to Him...to your father—" She cleared her throat. "Sorry, I mean Raimond, salvation was extended to you, your son, and as many as the Lord will call to Himself."

"It's all right, Sandra. Raimond will always be my father, but I'll always be Evan's Daddy's little girl."

"Thank you." Raimond struggled with his emotions that came from the lips of his only child. "Does this mean you've forgiven me?" he asked hopefully.

"It's a process," she told him. "But I want in on the promise God made to you."

When little Stephan stirred, Raimond became alarmed and quickly handed him back to his daughter.

Sandra chuckled and quietly slipped out the room.

Raimond loved that woman, because she was so in tune with his emotions, so this time, he let her leave. God's promises were true. Jesus told him to trust Him and he got a double—no, triple blessing—a daughter back, a grandson, and a hungry soul for the Lord.

Now, only one thing was missing from his life—a wife. And he had his eyes set on one—Sandra Nicholson would be his in ninety days or less.

Chapter

Twenty-One

"If we confess our sins, God is faithful and just to forgive us and to cleanse us from all unrighteousness," Pastor Rouse said as he began his Sunday morning sermon from 1 John 1:9.

Although he continued to insert other Scriptures into his message, Sandra's eyes hadn't budged past verse nine. Pastor Rouse was giving her the confirmation she needed to proceed. It wasn't a coincidence that she happened to be visiting Raimond's church on this day and heard this message.

After witnessing the spirit of peace that descended in the hospital waiting room the day Baby Stephan was born, Sandra had craved that total forgiveness... from others too.

Sitting next to Raimond, he had no idea the effect his reconciliation with Kelsi and her parents had on her. Neither did her sons and their families who were visiting Temple Church of Christ today too.

The service had been so emotional for her that tears blurred her vision during altar call as dozens made the decision to repent and accept the baptism of water and the Holy Ghost in Jesus' name.

"You okay?" Raimond whispered for her ears only after the benediction.

"Yes." She mustered a smile.

"And no." He frowned. "I see something in your eyes that contradicts those beautiful lips of yours." He reached for her hand and tugged her out the way of other members who were trying to walk around them. "Baby, we're beyond secrets, so if anything is bothering you—"

"I'll let you know." Sandra gathered her thoughts and purse. "Come on. I have the meal ready to serve."

Next to shopping, Sandra enjoyed cooking for her family and she had prepared a great meal for them. It relaxed her and she needed that today as she timed her day to make her announcement to all until everyone had finished their dessert.

So less than an hour later after Raimond said grace, her family enjoyed her cooking with little conversation among the men.

"How's little Stephan?" Eva asked as she complained about the summer heat in the latter stages of her pregnancy.

"He's perfect," Raimond boasted, then rested his fork on the table.

That was one fork down, Sandra counted. Talise and Eva were always the last to finish, because, guilty like her, they nibbled, talked, and nibbled some more.

Relax, she coaxed herself, *and enjoy the moment.* After all, Sandra had never seen Raimond so happy than when he talked about his grandson.

"As a matter of fact, Kelsi has two more weeks, and the doctor says she can resume her normal activities."

Eva chuckled, then took a sip of milk. "The last time we talked, she said she was going to do some grants writing to get more funding for the museum."

"Yes." Raimond's expression seemed reflective, then he cleared his throat. "I never thought I would see this day— Kelsi speaking to me, wanting to help me, and holding my grandson. Forgiveness does a soul good." He reached for Sandra's hand. "And most importantly, gave me a woman that God had hidden among the pearls."

Sandra blushed under his attention, but this moment wasn't for sentimental toasts as "Amens" floated around the table. Besides, the only person still eating was Kidd who was on his second helping of key lime pie. "The Jamieson family reunion is coming up, isn't it?" she asked.

Ace nodded and reached for more punch for Lauren, who was growing impatient by patting her hands on the table.

"Good, I think I'll tag along this time." She slipped a serving of dessert in her mouth and refused to make eye contact with anyone, anticipating her guests' stunned expressions. Even Eva and Talise didn't back her.

"It's a Jamieson reunion," Kidd stated slowly.

"I know that." Sandra shrugged coolly, but her heart pounded with the unknown reception she might receive. "Grandma BB has already gone twice and she's not a Jamieson."

Kidd rubbed his neck. "Yeah, but there's no sense in arguing with that woman about that. She's itching for target practice, looking for any reason for someone to cross her. I heard her trial for assault was a sight to see, but I don't want to see it. Eva and I know firsthand the damage she can cause, even as a stroke victim."

"Yes, we do," Eva mumbled.

"She's all bark and no bite." Sandra felt Raimond watching her.

"Why now, Mom? You were adamant that the reunion shouldn't include you. What has changed?" Talise's eyebrows were knitted together.

"Babe?" Raimond finally spoke as her hand trembled under his strong one. Their eyes met and Sandra saw his confusion. "What's going on?"

Sandra stalled. Surely, he would understand. Once she swallowed, she glanced to her sons, then explained, "I've wronged your half-siblings. I owe their mother an apology. The sermon today confirmed my decision. I guess the reunion is neutral ground for that."

The groans echoed around her.

"I forbid it," Kidd roared, then cowered under twisted lips. "Sorry...I mean, I don't think that's a good idea, Ma. Eillian Jamieson barely tolerates the sight of me and Ace. And there's no love lost between us either, but I'm respectful as you've reared us."

"Speak for yourself, bro," Ace corrected. "I think she likes me. Number one, I'm the cute one and you look more like Samuel than I do." Her youngest son winked, but his light joke lost the punch line.

Raimond lifted her hand to his lips and brushed a kiss on her knuckles. Worry was plastered on his face. "Babe, it sounds like you're going unnecessarily into a hostile environment."

"True." She was an outcast to the Jamieson family—she had been a mistress and never a wife. "I do have some allies. My sons' younger half-sister, Queen, is a sweetheart and is

179

always glad to see me whenever she visits her big brothers every now and then."

Although Kidd and Ace embraced Queen as their baby sister, the first set of Samuel's siblings weren't that easy to love. Again, their coolness was understandable. Surprisingly, all of Samuel's children were willing to mend distrusted hearts, and the reunion was one way to do it.

"I know Denise holds no harsh feelings against you, at least that's what she told Gabrielle," Talise said of Cameron's wife's best friend, whose maiden name was Jamieson. "I believe her, but Zaki is another story. He's worse than my brother-in-law when it comes to anger management issues." Talise grinned at Kidd, then squinted back at Sandra. "But what has God said?"

"I think He'll be with me, whether the first Mrs. Jamieson accepts my apology or not. I feel like it's time to tell her I'm sorry." The key word was "think." Sandra hoped it was God's will. She had been praying and felt the message that was preached was her sign.

"Great. Grandma BB will love this." Kidd hissed. "She's always looking for a reason to fire off that g-u-n."

"G-u-n?" Raimond stiffened and looked alarmed. "You mean she really is some kind of kin to Stagecoach Mary?"

"O*nuh.*" Raimond shook his head and pounded his fist on the table. "This is not happening without me. Add one more to the guest list. There's no way anyone's going to disrespect my lady."

Kidd smirked with amusement, then nodded at Raimond. "I like you a little bit more every day."

Any other time, Sandra would have blushed at Raimond's possessiveness, but not today. "I'm not going to war, you all.

I'm sure Eillian and I can have a civil conversation."

"Did you hear the last part of the sermon, Sandra?" Talise quizzed. *"For we wrestle not against flesh and blood, but against principalities, against powers, against the rulers of the darkness of this world, against spiritual wickedness in high places.'* Ephesians 6, so I think you better suit up."

Weeks later, Sandra was gazing out the window of Flight 13 to Birmingham, Alabama. Once there, her Jamieson clan would take the fifty-mile drive to Tuscaloosa, Alabama, to The Jemison-Van de Graaff.

The twenty-six room mansion was built for Senator Robert Jemison Jr., and considered a tourist attraction, since he was one of the largest slaveholders in Alabama with eight plantations and more than four hundred enslaved blacks. Despite the spelling variation, Parke explained his family shouldn't ignore a possible connection, because their Jamieson bloodline came from a man by the same name during slavery. Raimond agreed with him.

Sandra had only been to the mansion one time for Cameron and Gabrielle's wedding. Since then, the Jamiesons have held three reunions.

"Sweetheart." Raimond's voice invaded her thoughts. "Any idea on how many Jamiesons will attend?"

"No," she said softly, finding comfort in the compassion brimming from his eyes. "I overheard Parke say one hundred and fifty, maybe more."

"So is this Eillian woman coming?"

"I was told she did last time. All I know is she could've been looking for me?" Sandra released a laugh that she wasn't feeling. A woman scorned wouldn't be looking for her husband's mistress unless she had a delivery, usually fatal. "Thank you for not trying to talk me out of it. I love you for that."

"I love you too, but…" He leaned and pressed his lips to hers, then pulled back. Their lids fluttered open at the same time. "Baby, I'm not one hundred percent sold on this, but I'm here to support you in good times and bad."

His choice of phrasing temporarily distracted her. Those were forever and ever words. She had to stay focused. "She deserves an apology and so do her children." She pursed her lips. "I want to get this burden off my back."

"Well, I have your back," he said with a stern look. "You don't need Kidd or Grandma BB. The Lord sent me." He patted his chest.

She grinned, then turned and glanced out the window. Raimond left her to her thoughts for the rest of the flight. Between her prayers, which God hadn't uttered a whisper and her mantra of "Face your fears," Sandra was beginning to question her decision, even with backup.

Too soon, the plane landed and even sooner, they arrived at the host hotel.

Families climbed out, dragging suitcases, and the children ran circles around adults, playing. Hugs and kisses were exchanged and hearty greetings. The reunion had grown from just Samuel's children and their children. Thanks to Parke and Cameron, more descendants of Paki Kokumuo Jaja wanted to be included.

"Are you okay?" Raimond whispered as they strolled to the lobby of The Courtyard by Marriott.

Sandra couldn't speak, but nodded. *I do belong here,*

right? she asked herself. Although she had contributed two sons to the family tree, did she really fit?

After Raimond paid for his room, then hers, he grabbed her carry-on.

They were heading to the set of elevators when a sultry voice called Sandra's name.

Recognition was immediate as Sandra twirled around to see Queen Jamieson walking toward her. With her one-dimpled smile, Queen's arms were stretched wide open. If Sandra had had a daughter, she would wish that she was as beautiful and regal as Queen, who was properly named. Her dark skin glistened with good health and her long lashes were to envy. It didn't hurt that her figure was hand carved from the Master Craftsman.

Queen was radiant, vibrant, and possessed a calmness about her that made others relaxed. After her only sister died from cancer, she was determined to seek out and embrace all her siblings. With no shame, Queen forced her way into their lives whether they were cordial or not. She was the last offspring of Samuel Jamieson—to everyone's knowledge.

"It's good to see you again!" The girl gushed as they exchanged hugs. "I didn't know you were coming…" When she took a breath, she seemed to notice Raimond. Her lips formed an "o" before *wow* came out. "And you are?" Her eyes twinkled in mischief.

"Everything Sandra ever wanted and more, Raimond Mayfield." He shook Queen's hand.

Really? Sandra smirked as Queen batted her lashes at her.

"I like him." She pointed.

"Me too." Sandra winked.

"I am standing here, ladies," Raimond said, clearing his throat.

"You started it," Sandra teased. While Sandra chatted with Queen, Raimond didn't leave her side. He stood with his arms folded as if he was her paid bodyguard. All he needed was a trench overcoat and a Fedora, then he could play the part.

Once Sandra convinced Queen that her color scheme of bold and soft gold was flattering, the young woman left to greet other siblings.

Remembering Raimond's presence, Sandra faced him. "Sorry, Queen's energy is contagious. You didn't have to stay by me." Sandra reached for her luggage, but Raimond was faster.

"I can't let you go, Sandra. Never again."

She frowned. Were they talking about the same thing? she wondered as they rode the elevator to her floor. He made sure she was safe in her room, before he went to his.

As Sandra unpacked, she didn't plan to leave her room until the next day for breakfast. She would order room service, read her Bible, and pray for Eillian's forgiveness.

Chapter

Twenty-Two

Raimond knocked on Kidd's hotel room door. "Do you and your brother have a minute to have a word with me?"

"Sure, I'll call Ace."

They agreed on a place and met within minutes at the end of the hall in a small sitting area.

"What's up?" Taking a seat, Ace leaned back and crossed his ankle over his knee.

"Does this have to do with my mother?" Kidd asked, seemingly on guard.

Raimond nodded, took a deep breath, and stared them down. "I love Sandra. I plan to ask her to marry me, so I want your blessings."

Neither answered right away, then Ace spoke first. "My mother deserves a happiness that can't be measured, but the man who professes such a thing, I will measure it."

Expecting resistance from Kidd, Raimond was surprised by Ace's veil threat.

He waited for Kidd who had bowed his head and huffed. He continued to wait him out. Finally he looked up. His expression was blank.

"Like Ace, my mother's happiness is my utmost concern. I know how she feels about you and you know how I feel about you. Make her happy and we'll be happy. Make her cry and you won't be happy."

"As it should be." Praise God that was easy. Raimond had expected a tug of war or any other theatrics. Kidd was about to stand, but Raimond stopped him. "One more thing, I want us to pray for Sandra—and not from afar. I don't want her to be hurt."

"That's not going to happen." Kidd cracked his knuckles while Ace flexed his muscles.

"Don't let my gray hair fool you. Once a wrestler, I'm always a tackler." He grinned. "I thought you two might want to know that." They didn't seem fazed. "Anyway, I'm talking about spiritually. The hardest word to say in any language is sorry. I want to pray with her, but she has a Do Not Disturb sign on her door."

"I'm with you on this." Kidd stood and shook hands. We'll gather our wives and call Ma."

Ten minutes later, Raimond led Sandra's family into her suite, to her surprise. "What's this?"

Raimond kissed her. "Your prayer band." He smiled. "I sensed your anxiety. I can pray for you, but I'd rather do that with you."

The love that shone in her eyes made Raimond want to drop to one knee, but their time would come.

Nudging Sandra into the middle, Raimond instructed everyone to join hands. The adults complied. Her granddaughters, who were drugged with sleep, were placed on their Nani's bed.

"Father God, in the mighty name of Jesus, we come boldly to Your throne of grace where we might find mercy. Thank You for the blood You shed on Calvary for our sins, including Sandra's. Lord, we don't have the authority to declare anything that is not Your will, so Lord, please show us Your will and give the woman I love peace. In Jesus' name. Amen."

They rejoiced quietly and sang a few hymns, mindful of the girls and the hotel's thin walls. Sandra wrapped her arms around his waist and rested her head on his chest. She sniffed and buried her face in his shirt.

Throughout the rejoicing, Raimond heard her soft, *Thank you.*

"Always," he whispered back before everyone said their goodnights and left.

Sandra woke with a smile the next morning as she stretched. There was something sexy about a praying man and she was glad that he loved her enough to be in tune with her triumphs and fears.

After enjoying breakfast, family and friends loaded the bus for The Jemison-Van de Graaff Mansion minutes away. As Raimond slid in the seat next to her, Sandra rested her head on his shoulder. "Give the woman I love peace." All she could think about was the words from his prayer. Being in love was a good distraction.

Once at the picnic, seeking out Eillian was no longer her main focus and she clung to Raimond's side, sharing barbecue and playing with the grandchildren. Then Sandra spied Eillian under one of the shady old trees. She took a deep breath and exhaled. If the Lord told her to do this, then she was going to follow through.

"I'll be back," she whispered into Raimond's ear, but he only tightened his hold on her hand.

"Are you sure this is God?" His brown eyes bore into hers.

Sandra nodded and wiped her hands on a napkin. She counted to three and prayed as her shaky legs carried her in that direction. She weaved her way in and out of the crowd, exchanging smiles with her sons' relatives whose names were unknown to her.

With large dark glasses shielding Eillian's eyes from the sun, Sandra didn't know if the woman was watching her or not. Sandra kept going until she was within speaking distance.

"Hi, I'm—"

"I know who you are." The woman spat out the last word.

Not a good sign. Sandra's heart pounded as she took the seat next to her, then scanned the picnic area. Despite the buzz of activity, Sandra's world seemed to come to a stop as she gathered her words. Through the blur of the crowd, she recognized the faces of her beloved sons spying in her direction.

Gripping the arms of the metal folding chair, Sandra went for it. "Eillian, I'm here to say I'm sorry."

"It's a little too late for that," she stated without removing her glasses or facing Sandra.

Better late than never, Sandra wanted to say, but doubted Eillian would appreciate that logic. "I didn't know Samuel was married when I started dating him and had my first son."

"I guess you silly little women never think to ask."

Silly? Her flesh was put on notice to be ready for whatever, but her spirit tamed it. "I suspected that before my second son was born."

The woman turned and Sandra assumed she was staring at her, because she never removed her glasses. "*Miss Nicholson,* why are you talking to me about your shame?"

"I wanted to apologize," Sandra said softly. "To ask for your forgiveness and to let you know I've repented."

"Keep your apology. It's thirty plus years expired." She leaned forward. "You have a lot of nerve asking me to forgive you when you knew you were sleeping with a married man at some point in your relationship and tearing up a family. Each moment he stayed with you," she practically snarled, "was time away from his children and wife. Each dime he spent on you and your…" Sandra cringed at the profanity she called her sons, but she refused to take the bait as the woman ranted. "How do we get that back?"

Sandra had no answer as she looked away and saw Kidd, Ace, Parke, Cameron, and others in position, reminding her of a secret service detail. She blinked and realized Raimond was closer to her than them. She faced her foe again. "You can't. Your family can't, and for that I'm sorry."

"If you're done with your whining, you can take your sorry behind back to where you and your sons are."

Getting to her feet, Sandra squeezed her lips together. *Lord, what happened?* She had no mercy for me. She blinked away tears.

My yoke is easy and My burden is light, God whispered. *It's My forgiveness that counts.*

"Well, I'm sorry for disturbing you."

She sneered. "Didn't I tell you that I don't want your sorry! You messed with my Sam's head and he became worthless as a husband. Thanks to you!" She raised her voice and they became center stage. Before Sandra knew it, everyone was advancing as if they were clearing bases at a baseball game.

Just like Sandra had, his first wife saw no fault with Samuel. She wanted to tell the woman that her husband had started it, but did that make a difference now? It took two people to commit fornication.

"I told myself that if I ever came face-to-face with you in an alley or on the streets, I'd shoot you." She made a gesture but fell back in her chair. The woman wasn't bluffing. "If I didn't have this stroke I would get up and beat the snot out of you with my cane."

Sandra noticed the stick at the same time she felt a presence beside her.

"That's where you're wrong, Mrs. Jamieson. I understand this to be a family friendly event and she was only trying to be friendly, but it appears Sandra wasted her time."

Wrapping his arm around her waist, Sandra followed Raimond's lead as he steered her through the crowd. "Carry on," he told everybody along the path.

When Kidd and Ace tried to approach, Raimond shook his head. "Not now." Sandra was grateful they obliged.

She didn't realize tears were on her cheeks until she and Raimond were alone in a gazebo. Raimond held her without saying a word.

Finally, she emptied her well of tears mingled with sorrow, regret, anything but relief. Sandra sniffed, then cried again. Raimond was patient and waited until she was completely quiet, then kissed her hair. "Better?"

She nodded, then shook her head. "I don't know."

He squeezed her tight, then slowly loosened his embrace. "Sweetheart, can I speak or do you prefer I hold my peace?"

"Yes." She tilted her head and stared into his eyes.

"You can't tell your faults to just anybody and everybody. James 5:16 says, confess to one *another*, meaning those in the Body of Christ. By doing so, we can pray for each other and be spiritually healed of whatever sin is bothering us. God's timing is perfect and we have to be in His will."

"Do you think I wasn't in His will to apologize?"

He shrugged and rubbed his jaw against her hair. "I don't know. Outside of Believers, some people will forgive you, others won't in a lifetime. As saints of God, when we transgress against each other, the Bible tells us in Matthew 5:23 to reconcile with them before coming to Him. That's how we're spiritually healed." He rubbed her arm. "We'll never know if our apologies will lead them to Christ in our lifetime."

She snuggled into his chest. His heartbeat was strong. "Amen." Listening to Raimond's steady heartbeat gave Sandra so much peace. "And one more thing."

"What's that, babe?"

"I don't think I'm going to crash another family reunion."

Raimond's laugh was infectious and Sandra caught it and joined in.

Chapter Twenty-Three

"I've been thinking," Kelsi whispered as she cuddled her son in her arms and Stephan wrapped his arms around both of them. They were lounging around the house and content at doing nothing, but talk about the baby, their dreams, and their goals in life.

"About?" he prompted.

"I want to start going back to church."

Stephan kissed her forehead. "I've been thinking about that too, ever since we attended that grand opening. There is too much ugly stuff in this world."

"Raimond trusted God that I would come around, and despite all my bitterness and meanness, I did." she shrugged. "Maybe, because I know deep down inside I want that much faith in God to protect our son."

"Great minds think alike, babe."

Kelsi grinned. "I'm glad I married you."

"I'm glad I asked." Stephan wiggled his eyebrows. "I

know a sweet thang when I see one."

The following Sunday, they made their son's official outing at six weeks a going-to-church affair, inviting their parents and Kelsi's siblings. She decided to attend the church where Raimond worshiped, since she really didn't have a connection anymore with her childhood congregation. Raimond had been ecstatic with the news. It felt good to know she had made his day.

Both families gathered at her home and before everyone left, her parents pulled her aside. "I'm glad you've forgiven Raimond," her mother said.

Kelsi nodded. "I haven't forgotten, but the bitterness was too heavy a burden to carry."

"Raimond might not have been around when you were a girl, but he has made one contribution to the family," her father said.

"What?" Kelsi asked hesitantly, eying them with suspicion.

"He managed to get the Coleman and Edwards households to go to church," her mother said in a reflective tone.

"I guess so." Kelsi hadn't thought of it that way. Maybe he was good for something.

Following the guidance of their GPS, Stephan led the pack into the church parking lot half an hour later. Kelsi stared at the pristine white structure and frowned.

"What, babe?" Stephan asked as he was about to get out.

She blinked, but couldn't take her eyes off the building. "It just hit me. I can't remember when, why, or for what reason I stopped going to church." She strained her mind for the answer as Stephan came around to her side of the door and assisted her out, then reached for their sleeping infant as Tyler screeched to a stop in the space next to them with Lindsay in the passenger seat. The others weren't far behind.

As they walked closer to the entrance, Kelsi was amused to see Raimond pacing the foyer. He stopped when he saw her. He beat the ushers opening the door for her and her entourage.

Whenever he had visited her, Raimond had a humble spirit about himself, which was such a contrast to when she first saw him at the museum where he eluded such great confidence.

She noticed he was always careful with what he said and his actions as if fearing that she would take away his undeserving right to see Baby Stephan. Her heart began to ache for him and when he talked about the museum, she decided to use some of her expertise as a grant writer for the school district to help him. She had almost cried, witnessing his emotional happiness when she told him.

"Handsome," Raimond said in an awe-like tone. "May I carry him?" He looked hopeful, glancing from Kelsi to Stephan.

Kelsi consented and they trailed him to where Sandra greeted everyone and cooed at the baby. Through Eva's eyes, Kelsi saw why Sandra was so likable. The woman was genuine, period, and Kelsi doubted she would ever forget what Sandra said the day Baby Stephan... Sandra had quietly left the hospital room; Kelsi supposed to give her and Raimond some bonding time. Her return seemed to be timed to when Raimond had walked out the room to take an important call from D.C.

Sandra's eyes had been so kind when she whispered, *"I know I represent the type of woman that pulled your family apart and on behalf of women who have acknowledged their sins and repented, please forgive us."*

Kelsi's eyes watered. Raimond and Sandra's honesty had tugged at her, but she said nothing.

"You didn't have to let your father—Raimond—" she quickly corrected, *"be a part of your special day. I don't know if that means you've forgiven him or not..."*

She hadn't, but at that moment, the process started. Kelsi's mind returned to the present. She didn't want to dwell on the past, but wanted to see what was there for her today.

Once everyone was settled in their seats, Kelsi and Stephan held hands and seemed to exhale together as they scanned their surroundings. The sanctuary was neither mega large or cozy small, just the right size to feel at home among hundreds.

The praise singers' music selections were slow and soothing, which gave her peace. Finally, the minister approached the pulpit and welcomed visitors. He made a few announcements, then began his sermon to Kelsi's relief. Since this was their first outing with the baby, she didn't know how long her son would remain asleep.

"I want you to look around you and see how many children are among us," Pastor Rouse requested.

At the same time, Kelsi and Stephan glanced at their baby and smiled. Raimond seemed so content and peaceful to hold his grandson.

"God wants us to come to Him, as children, for everything. We must be humble, honor and respect Him as the person in charge, and trust and believe that He is an all-knowing God like our children believe we—as parents—know everything."

The preacher had Kelsi's attention.

"Matthew 18:3-4 talks about children in a way that is our spiritual example to come to Christ—humble. Pride will disqualify you from heaven. Pride is as stubborn as a weed among flowers. It is to be despised. It will keep you from loving and forgiving."

Sucking in her breath, Kelsi's heart pounded. *He's talking about me,* she thought.

"Some of you may think humility means weakness." He shook his head. "Jesus didn't lose any power on the cross...but back to the children. Mothers, fathers, we won't stand for anyone to mess with our kids—we won't do it. How do you think God feels about someone messing with His own children? The retribution is swift. Put it this way, you don't want to get on the Lord's bad side. The Bible says He will avenge our enemies."

Kelsi thought about the images she saw in Raimond's museum; they were brutal, hateful, and alarming, yet this sermon gave her comfort that God would avenge those who depended on Him as children. Somehow, knowing that did lessen the hate racists had provoked. Now, she understood the pity toward them her father had wanted the narrator to leave with visitors.

The sermon was so intense that Kelsi was almost on the edge of the pew with Stephan squeezing her hand. When little Stephan stirred, Lindsay volunteered to take him to the ladies' room and change his diaper to Kelsi's relief. She didn't want to miss anything, but when the pastor closed his Bible, Kelsi was disappointed. She wanted to hear more.

"Will the congregation please stand." He waited as everyone got on their feet. "Here's the first step toward being

Christ's child. Repent now. It's not required that you confess your sins to anyone but Him—He knows them anyway. Then come to the altar for prayer and complete the plan of salvation with the water baptism in Jesus' name to bleach those spiritual sins away. It's God's promise to fill you with the fire of the Holy Ghost if you repent and turn your back on sin. The evidence is outlined in the entire Book of Acts..."

While Kelsi asked God for forgiveness for whatever she had done wrong, including the way she had treated her father, Stephan nudged her.

"Want to do this together, babe?" he whispered and gave her an encouraging smile.

She sighed, wishing she could gather her son and they all could take this journey together.

His time will come.

There was no other voice so strong that Kelsi couldn't recognize it as God's. Nothing could stop her now. She nodded. "Yes."

Applause was deafening as if the sanctuary had swelled into a sports arena when they entered the aisle with others. She never imagined this humility thing made her a rock star, but there she and Stephan were, surrounded by people who were cheering them on, crying, and lifting up their hands.

Stephan loosened her hand, then slipped his arm around her waist for the rest of the journey to the front. In unison, as if they were exchanging their vows again, they told the minister they had repented and wanted the works of salvation.

That's when she and Stephan were separated and shown to dressing rooms where they changed out of their church clothes for white garments for their baptism. The helpers honored her request that she and her husband be baptized together, so at the entrance to the pool, Kelsi faced Stephan in a white T-shirt, pants, and socks standing on the other side. He gave her a thumbs up. Kelsi blew him a kiss as two ministers held out their hands and assisted them into the water.

Kelsi took a deep breath as the two ministers instructed Kelsi and Stephan to cross their arms over their chests, then one of the ministers raised his arm.

"My dear brother and sister, upon the confession of your faith and the confidence that we have in the death, burial, and grand resurrection of our Lord and Savior Jesus Christ, we indeed baptize you in His name, the Lord Jesus Christ, for the remission of your sins—Acts 4:12 says, 'Neither is there salvation in any other, for there is no other name under heaven given among men, whereby we must be saved.' God will baptize you with fire of the Holy Ghost."

Their submersion under water was swift, but so was their reemergence.

Tears mixed with water streamed down Kelsi' face and she turned to her husband. As the crowd rejoiced, Stephan reached out and they hugged each other, crying. "Every thing's going to be all right..." Stephan began but then the unexplainable happened. His words sounded funny, its language was unfamiliar, and the atmosphere seemed to change. As the ministers tried to separate them to guide them out the pool, Kelsi held on tighter, and soon that same power embraced her and she and Stephan were rejoicing, speaking to God in an unknown language. While under this influence, Kelsi was led out of the water and back into the dressing room.

Things were a blur as Kelsi dried off and changed back

into her clothes, then joined other baptismal candidates who were rejoicing and praying in a small chapel. Stephan was also there, clapping and praising God. Kelsi went to him and hugged him. Together they worshiped God with everything that was within them.

Soon, her family appeared. Her mother was holding Baby Stephan, who was alert.

"Do you know how many diaper changes your baby has gone through?" Lindsay teased, but looked confused about what Kelsi had just experienced.

She and Stephan were zapped of their physical energy as they slumped in chairs. An older woman, who seemed to be in charge, explained what happened and welcomed them into the body of Christ.

"I want my baby to be saved," Kelsi said in a weak voice.

The woman identified as Sister Green nodded and her eyes sparkled. "The promise of salvation is to anyone who the Lord should call. There will be a time where your baby will become a man and know the difference between right and wrong."

This woman wasn't privy to what God had told her earlier. Yet, Sister Green had confirmed it.

"Until then," the woman continued, "you can bring him back next Sunday and the pastor will bless your child, the parents, and family to help him walk in the way of the Lord and never depart from it."

Almost in unison her family answered, "We'll be here."

"Amen." Kelsi beamed as she cuddled her son in her arms and Stephan announced he was starved.

"This calls for a celebration," Raimond shouted with teary eyes as he led the way out the church, rejoicing.

Chapter
Twenty-Four

Sandra never believed in dreams coming true, but she had complete confidence in God answering prayers. And that seemed to be her problem. Raimond Mayfield had stepped out of a woman's dreams into her life. It wasn't that she hadn't thought about a mate, but Sandra just hadn't prayed for one, so where did that leave her with Raimond?

They had professed their "I love you's" some time ago, but where did they go from there, considering God had answered Raimond's prayers?

What was the dating protocol these days anyway? Six months of dating, engaged three months, then a wedding a year later?

If Sandra didn't stop frowning at her reflection in the mirror, her eyeliner wouldn't find a straight line.

Finally, the task was complete, and Sandra scrutinized the new brand of makeup Talise had talked her into purchasing. Next her daughter-in-law insisted on giving her a new style—

an updo—for a drop-dead gorgeous look. Sandra chuckled. Talise had no shame in admitting that the recent makeover was to make Sandra turn heads, which she did, including Raimond's, but it hadn't changed their dating status.

Walking out of the bathroom, she wiggled her toenails, accessing the pedicure she enjoyed with her daughters-in-law before slipping into her heels. She liked the quirky shade of green against her skin tone, and the pairing with her silver dress was complementary.

Her thoughts returned to Raimond. They were over the four-month mark of dating. Her parents had been married for forty years. Would Sandra ever reach half that milestone and would it be with Raimond? "What are you waiting on?" she said out loud. "We're in our fabulous fifties, not 'take our time twenties.' " She sighed, wanting to tell him that, then a Scripture came to mind. *Love is patient...* 1 Corinthians 13:4.

She couldn't argue with God, so Sandra had no choice but to shut out her doubts.

Raimond's ringtone chimed as if he knew he was on her mind.

"Are you ready?" Raimond asked when Sandra answered the phone.

"Ready and waiting." *In more ways than one*, she thought again about a forever.

"What are you wearing?" It sounded like he cooed to her and she responded with a blush.

"The dress you requested."

Today was about a celebration with Baby Stephan getting blessed before morning service. Kelsi wanted to take photos and Raimond wanted her to match him in light gray attire.

"I don't want us to be the last ones there for the pictures, so I'm getting out of my car and walking to your door and eagerly waiting for a kiss as you fix my tie—"

"You're here?" Sandra hurried to peek out the window. She hadn't heard his car drive up.

Sandra opened her door and admired his swagger as if he was on a catwalk, especially with the cell phone at his ear. She sucked in her breath, liking the designer single-breasted, two-button suit she had selected for him and made him model it more than once just so she could indulge in his handsomeness. She had chosen the gray suit and waited while he tried it on. Where was his teal tie?

She exhaled. Raimond had the type of looks that would probably last until he was ninety-plus. Whenever she saw him, it was like the first time they met and she watched as he generously gave appreciative glances.

"Bye, darling. See you in three, two, one..." He disconnected and clipped his phone back on his waist belt. "Hi." His eyes twinkled with mischief. "I like what I see."

So did she and that was the source of her melancholy. She was ready for more and he wasn't. Sandra stepped back so he could enter.

"Good morning."

Her lids fluttered to receive his hug and kiss. She wished it could be like this every day between them.

When she pulled away, his eyes seemed to smother as he studied her, then began to name all the things he liked about her. "You have the most beautiful hair, it's thick and long. I'm glad you haven't cut it." He fingered it.

Sandra had thought about it a few times during the summer, but Talise wouldn't hear of it. She fussed that women half her age bought synthetic hair to boast what God had already given Sandra.

"Your eyes and smile are my undoing. They tell me things about you."

Don't look at him, don't look at him, don't look at him. Otherwise, Sandra feared that he would see the pleading in her eyes that she wanted and was ready to be Mrs. Mayfield. She was about to tell him to stop when he mentioned her passion.

"I've learned so much from you, and it isn't limited to your love for fashion. It's what you create with the tools you have: confidence, inner beauty…"

"You're going to make me cry," she choked out.

"I'm here to catch them." His loving gaze made her love him even more. "Plus, can I help it if you're my distraction?" He reached for her hand. "Come on."

Did his voice lower to a bass quality like Barry White? She grabbed her purse and locked her front door.

"We better hurry, sweetheart, so we can get in on the picture-taking with my grandson." He grinned.

"Now, you're sure that Kelsi wants me in this *family* photo?"

"Yes, she knows you're a sweet lady and she wants both of us to be happy." He winked, then escorted to his SUV in almost a speed walk trek.

While Raimond drove, Sandra reminisced about when her granddaughters were blessed. There were so many Jamiesons in attendance; they could have formed their own spin-off church.

Twenty minutes later, when Raimond arrived at Temple Church of Christ, there was a small group congregating in the parking lot not far from the door. Families on both sides showed up for the grand occasion.

Sandra spoke to those who she knew and discreetly stayed in the background as Kelsi requested several poses. When she asked for the grandparents, Ivy and Evanston were first, followed by Stephan's parents.

It was a touching moment when Kelsi asked for Raimond, because she knew he wouldn't assume he had the right. It was heartwarming to see their relationship flourish little by little as Kelsi warmed up to Raimond taking baby steps in her life.

"Sandra, I want you in there too," Kelsi demanded with a hand on her hip.

"Me?" Sandra verified and complied.

Although Sandra accepted the gesture, she felt uncomfortable to pose with Raimond and his grandson when she wasn't even a longtime family friend. If she and Raimond parted ways and people looked at the photo, Sandra would be "that woman" who *had* been in family photos. Sandra had been a "that woman" before and she didn't want that title ever again.

Stephan checked his watch. "Sweetie, we have to hurry. The pastor wants to bless the baby before the sermon starts."

The group of close to twenty rushed toward the doors. Inside, the ushers did their best to seat them together and once everyone was situated, the pastor called the Edwards family. Sandra smiled. The man had no idea what it took to get them seated.

"Saints, I don't know if you all were here last week, but the parents of this baby submitted to the Lord and were baptized in Jesus' name." The congregation responded with applause. "I have seen many husbands and wives be baptized before, but I have never witnessed a more touching scene of surrender."

Sandra agreed as Amens echoed across the sanctuary. Stephan and Kelsi, cuddling the sleeping baby, led the way to the altar, followed by both families. The organist played a melody of "Jesus Loves the Little Children" as the ministers surrounded them.

After the pastor tabbed Holy Oil on the baby's head, he began to pray for Baby Stephan and everyone joined in. "Father, in the Name of Jesus, thank You for Stephan Evanston Raimond Edwards. Jesus, we ask that You send Your angels to guard and watch over him against the devil's tactics of violence, sexual immorality, illnesses, and more. Bless the household with praying parents, grandparents, and friends."

Sandra liked to hear ministers pray as if they were repeating the words that God gave them.

"In Jesus' name. Amen," the pastor concluded and kissed the baby's forehead before handing him back to Stephan, then the family returned to their seats.

After the choir belted out two songs, Pastor Rouse preached about overcoming every sin for Heaven's sake.

"My message today is the rewards of overcoming as stated in *Revelation 21:7: He that overcomes shall inherit all things; and I will be his God, and he shall be my son.*"

Although Raimond preferred she share his Bible when they attended church together, he never prohibited her from scribbling notes in the columns of his as she would her own. She had to, especially when the pastor cited the verses in chapter two and three.

Too soon, he closed his Bible and extended the altar call. Almost all of Kelsi and Stephan's family members walked down the aisle for prayer, and some of them requested the baptism of water and fire in Jesus' name, including Raimond's former wife and her husband.

She held Raimond's hand as they witnessed Ivy and Evan repent and have their sins washed away in Jesus' name.

Sandra choked back tears. *This is what salvation is all about,* she mused. Redemption.

The congregation was going crazy as one after another candidates were baptized. Others received the gift of the Holy Ghost with the evidence stated in Acts and some gave testimonies. When the pastor dismissed, many in the congregation continued their high praise and rejoicing. It was as if nobody wanted to leave.

"Let's all go to late lunch," Kelsi said afterward. Her face beamed with such happiness.

That sounded like a great idea to Sandra. She was starved.

Raimond kissed Kelsi's cheek and shook Stephan's hands. "You go on without us, sweetie."

Kelsi's pout had to mirror Sandra's because her stomach protested.

"Are you sure, Raimond? Stephan's doing a head count," his daughter countered. "There's plenty of room for you and Sandra."

"I'm sure. Thanks for including us."

She hoped Raimond was taking her somewhere nice to eat and soon. It had been a long service and folks didn't waste time exiting the sanctuary.

Linking his fingers through hers, Raimond tugged her in the opposite direction toward the altar.

"Babe, I think the deacons are ready to lock up," she whispered.

He didn't answer as he slipped his other hand in his

pocket and stared at the vacant pulpit, choir stand, and the baptismal pool. He appeared deep in thought, so she stayed quiet. If he was in commune with Jesus, who was she to interrupt?

When Raimond turned her around, she thought they were leaving, so she gathered her purse and his Bible. Instead, he steered her to a pew.

Come on. Her stomach whined, *I'm hungry*, but she sensed something deeper, spiritual had Raimond's attention, so she stilled the voice of protest.

Once they were seated, he draped an arm around her shoulders and pulled her closer. Resting her head on his shoulder, Sandra tried to tap into the place where his mind was.

The overhead lights dimmed in the sanctuary, creating streaks of sunlight to peer through the windows and gather at the tongue of fire emblem on the podium. She strained her ears to identify the music filtering through the speakers.

How appropriate the song was "At the Cross." Closing her eyes, Sandra hummed the words to the hymn.

"When I'm in the presence of God." Raimond ceased her mind from drifting. "It seems like yesterday when I came down an aisle and fell on my knees, repenting, asking God to forgive me and to save me." He paused. "Every time I come into God's house, kneel, and bow my head, it's like a renewal of me saying, 'Yes, Lord, I love You and I'm still committed to You. My relationship with Jesus is fresh.' "

Sandra smiled. Who could separate a man from his God? She thought about parts of Romans 8:35: S*hall tribulation, or distress, or persecution, or famine, or nakedness, or peril, or sword?*

"It seems like yesterday when I met you." His voice softened with the same awe he used when talking about their Savior. Sandra didn't interrupt him. "Actually, it's been almost five months of loving you, so here I am again." Raimond stirred.

Sandra opened her eyes and met him watching her as he slid off the pew. Her heart crashed against her chest.

"Getting on my knees. Lord, this time, I'm submitting myself to this woman that I'm asking You for."

Her hand trembled as he reached for it. "I'm committed to God and I want to be committed to you, Sandra Nicholson, to be faithful and cherish you, to be your boyfriend, the love of your life…your husband. Will you marry me?" He pulled a ring box out of his pocket and flipped open the lid. "When I met you, I asked if you belonged to any man. I want this diamond to make a statement that you now belong to this man."

The colors of hue in the sparkling cluster of diamonds caused *Yes* to get stuck in her throat as her eyes watered, so she nodded.

"God is our witness, Sandra, and He knows our hearts, but my ears need to hear you say yes."

"Yes," she whispered, then repeated in a stronger voice, "Yes."

Raimond slid on the ring and leaped up, pumped his fists in the air. He lifted her off her feet into the aisle and literally carried her out of the sanctuary and didn't stop until they were at his SUV in the parking lot.

Giggling, Sandra held on. "Raimond Mayfield, what's wrong with you?"

"There's no way I'm about to smooch my beloved

passionately in God's house." He grinned, then released her, so her feet touched the ground at the same time he deactivated his alarm and kissed her.

In his embrace, Sandra's eyes misted. *Lord, thank You for answering an unspoken prayer.* "Raimond?"

"Hmmm?"

"I'm hungry. Will you now feed your beloved?"

Laughing, Raimond assisted her in the passenger seat and they were on their way.

Chapter

Twenty-Five

"Deal with it, Mrs. Soon-to-be Mayfield," was Raimond's response three days later when Sandra balked at his request that they have a short engagement—real short.

Sandra rested her fist on her hips outside one of his exhibits at the museum and tried to be annoyed with his demand, but she couldn't. He wanted her as much as she wanted to be his, but still she had demands. "I want this day to be special."

Raimond guided her across the hall out of the way from volunteers who were removing two exhibits from his Juneteenth grand opening. One would coincide with a back-to-school theme by featuring historically black colleges.

So far, he had Dace creating a table-size replica of Cheyney University of Pennsylvania, the first historically black college in the United States, founded by a Quaker philanthropist almost thirty years before the end of slavery.

The exhibits Raimond chose always fascinated Sandra,

and she absorbed the wealth of information like an eager student. One unknown fact she learned as she watched the crew hang banners of historically black colleges was the large number of colleges and universities established for blacks, especially during slavery. She was also surprised at more than one hundred HBCUs still operating today compared to the ones that were now defunct.

"As long as you marry me, it will be special," Raimond said, pulling her mind away from the activity going on around them.

She blinked, almost forgetting her argument. Then she remembered. "Honey, it takes time to secure a venue, caterer, order a dress—"

"Shh." He placed a finger against her lips. "We can have the wedding at the museum. You said so yourself that the spiral stairwell is a majestic centerpiece."

"Did I say that?"

"You were thinking it." He tapped his lips on hers. "As for the dress." He grinned mischievously. "You can wear your pajamas and I'll still marry you."

"That ain't' happening."

"Didn't you say Eva likes to dabble in planning events?"

"Yes, but my daughter-in-law is very, very pregnant!" she argued. Sandra was becoming annoyed that her husband-to-be wasn't taking this most important event in their lives seriously.

"That's reason enough for us to hurry before she delivers, babe."

Squinting, Sandra did her best not to laugh, but when her fiancé released a snicker, she was a goner and agreed to his request as he walked her to her car, watched as she buckled up and then waved goodbye as she drove away.

The next day, Sandra was sitting in her dining room with her daughters-in-law overwhelmed as Eva grinned from ear to ear.

"I've been waiting for this day!" Eva snapped her fingers. "Don't worry about the food. There's a brother and sister catering company in North St. Louis—good food and good prices. Ooh, I know the perfect place to find African American cake toppers and…"

Sandra shook her head. Eva was like a pregnant woman on steroids as she mused through invitations that guaranteed a two-day turnaround. "Sweetie, have you forgotten that you're pregnant? And you're due in forty-five days or sooner like Kelsi."

Talise stopped turning the pages in a wedding planner catalog. "Evidently, you've forgotten that your sons are married to Jamieson women and we know how to throw a party—speaking of which, Grandma BB won the coin toss to host your wedding shower—" the three women groaned, "—and make this a major production."

"As it should be." Eva beamed as she shifted in her seat. Seconds later, all eyes were on her stomach as the baby stretched under her top.

"So you still don't know if you're having a boy or girl?" Sandra asked.

"Eva shook her head and grinned. "It would serve my husband right to have twin boys, since I'm a twin, and they could carry on the Jamieson name just to irk them.

"One day, he really will learn that it's not the name that makes the man, but the character of the man who makes his own name."

"Mom," Talise said softly. "You worry about the dress, tux, and cake." When Eva nodded, Talise continued, "I think among all the wives, we can take care of the invitations since you want it small, the food, music…"

"The honeymoon is in Mr. Mayfield's hands." Eva grinned. "Now, back to your wedding shower."

"All this in thirty days," Sandra mumbled, then listened to the devil in the details when it came to Grandma BB.

Two weeks later, Sandra arrived at Grandma BB's house early, only to find sparse parking. She was about to drive around the corner when she came upon two orange cones in front of the woman's mini mansion, as if someone was about to parallel park for their driver's test. Chippanddale strolled outside and waved for her to stop. At least he was wearing a shirt with his bow tie and sported a chauffeur's hat on his shaved head.

"Bea told me to park your car," he said when she lowered her window.

"And you need two clones for that?"

He laughed. "You know that was her idea of V.I.P parking."

After relinquishing her vehicle, she headed up the pathway to be met by another one of Grandma BB's boy toys to escort her up the steps. Sandra always thought the woman had good taste in men. If God sent a new millennium Azusa Street Revival to this woman's house, the church would be overtaken with good Christian men to do His bidding.

Inside the entrance was a long red carpet that led from the front door to a majesty chair like the one at Raimond's museum. There had to be among thirty-something ladies, including Kelsi?

Sandra was touched. Was she there because Eva had invited her or because she genuinely wanted to be included?

Building relationships take time, God whispered in her ear.

So Sandra stopped questioning her presence, but accepted it at face value. When Kelsi waved, Sandra smiled at her.

Now back to that monstrosity of a chair. Now where did she get that? Sandra learned when she first met the unofficial grandma of this family, not to ask questions.

"Wow, everybody. I guess I got the wrong memo on the start time." Sandra eyed Eva, then she sat in the chair, which swallowed her up with the softness of the cushion.

"Welcome to your shower and your pre-wedding rehearsal." Grandma BB whistled. Six men entered from the kitchen, their steps in sync like an army drill. Again, shirts covered their otherwise bared chests. They served guests appetizers of fruits, veggie, meat, various brown breads, and delicious dessert.

"The food is from the caterer Eva and I chose," Talise said. "As you can imagine, the presentation was all Grandma BB."

Their hostess swung one leg over a knee, then changed position and swung the other leg. She said nothing but guilt was smeared all over her face.

Next came the melodious sounds of an all-female string quartet. Lovely. If they had left the musical entertainment up to Grandma BB, there would have been a marching high school band.

While some ladies teased their servers, Sandra and the others ate.

Soon Grandma BB stood. "Chile, I hope you've enjoyed

yourself. I wanted to play some games, but Heney threatened me." She glared across the room and cut her eyes at Parke's wife, Cheney.

"Yes, because this crazy lady wanted to take this party to a whole new level with her Temptation game, but we began to pray and she conceded to let Talise pick a game."

"Party crasher," Grandma BB snapped and took her seat. She folded her arms and feigned an attitude, but it was all for show.

Talise sprang to her feet. "Anyone who wasn't sure what to get you, we suggested gift cards, since you were born to shop." She chuckled, then held up a basket decorated with bows the fall colors of her wedding, navy blue and blush. This basket will also serve as a wishing well at your wedding."

Whoever intertwined the blue and rose satin ribbons should go into business, Sandra mused.

"So we're going to play Ask Me About My Man before you open your gifts and cards, then whoever wants to give words of inspiration, we'll do that last."

Sandra made herself more comfortable. She liked to talk about Raimond to anyone who would give her five minutes. "Okay. I'm ready."

Grandma BB got up and clicked the heels of her Stacy Adams as if she was Dorothy in the old film, *The Wizard of Oz.* "I'll go first. You know I'm seventy-something." She ran her fingers through her silver platinum curls while others snickered. Sandra doubted the woman would ever tell her age. "There is still hope for me to snag a fine young man. You know I've turned down quite a few proposals from my boy toys."

Cheney got to her feet. "It's not that type of party,

Grandma. Can you stick to the game?" She gritted her teeth and sent some silence message, which made Grandma BB *hmph.* "You're not the boss of me." She jutted her chin. "Anyway, does he have his full set of teeth, pass gas, or doze off in the middle of a conversation? How much medication is he on, is he in shape, is his clothes in proportion with his weight and height?" Cheney and her sister-in-law, Hallison, made their way behind Grandma BB and gently but forcefully urged her back into her seat.

Shaking her head, Cheney chuckled. "Feel free to pass on any of her questions that make you uncomfortable, if you can remember them."

"I don't know how old you think Raimond is…"

"Fifty-five," Kelsi shouted and others joined her laughing, including Sandra.

"My husband-to-be has a beautiful set of teeth, and always has a smile for me. I think his gallbladder works properly, because I don't recall being in the midst of smelling polluted air." She thought about the other questions. "Raimond gives me his full attention and finishes all his sentences, he's in good health, and shape…and his clothes fit." To flame Grandma BB's naughtiness, she added, "Remember, I have dressed him," Sandra teased while guests whooped and crackled. "Not literally, but professionally."

"Then I guess there's hope for me. You know if Raimond had seen me first, you wouldn't have had a chance." Grandma BB nodded and folded her arms.

Sandra had to wipe a tear from her eye before responding. "I'm glad he didn't."

"For those who don't know how Mom and Raimond met, you've got to tell them," Talise insisted and Sandra obliged.

More questions followed and Sandra answered them thoughtfully. The game had served as a reflection of why she loved him.

Kelsi lifted her hand and asked, "Sandra, do you think you and my fath—Raimond—are soul mates? If so, how long would you have waited for him to get his act together, because you know he is kinda slow." She laughed and Sandra nodded her agreement.

"I couldn't agree more." It was okay to slip, Sandra wanted to encourage Kelsi about calling Raimond her father. He would be so honored.

Tilting her head, Sandra thought hard before answering. "I don't know if I believe in the whole soul mate thing, but I can say he is the love of my life. I do believe in God's hidden blessings. And God hid us from each other until the right time." She rested a hand on her chest. "You were the true blessing, Kelsi. God used you to bring us together and I will always thank you for allowing him back into your life."

Kelsi's eyes became glassy as she stood and maneuvered between guests to her and Sandra got on her feet. They met halfway and hugged. "Thank you for coming into his life, Sandra. Love you."

Tears flowed as Sandra kissed her cheek. "I love you too."

Awws floated among the guests until the two were swallowed up in a group hug. It was a memorable moment, even when Grandma BB shoved her way in, stating, "Coming through."

Her timing couldn't be better as Cheney called an impromptu prayer meeting and they wouldn't let her escape.

After the Amens, Eva asked guests not to leave if they had words of encouragement.

"Before you do that," Sandra said. "I would like to thank everyone for coming. I know I'm at this place, because of the Jamieson women around me who prayed for a mate. Honestly, I'm nervous about becoming a wife. Age isn't a factor. I want to readjust my needs and honor my husband's—" she shook her head, "—which is why I'm getting married in two weeks instead of two months, but I want to be a good wife and have a good marriage."

"You will," echoed around her as more than a few shared words of encouragement.

As the party came to a close, Sandra could hear the voice of God, sharing His inspiration, *Two are better than one, because they have a good reward for their labor: For if they fall, the one will lift up his fellow; but woe to him that is alone when he falls, for he hath not another to help him up.*

Sandra smiled, recognizing the familiar passage in Ecclesiastes 4. As two wounded, but redeemed souls, God gave them each other to hold the other up. Amen.

Chapter

Twenty-Six

Sandra knew what she was getting herself into, so why was she nervous to become Raimond's wife? *Because you're about to make a vow until death do you part,* she reminded herself as she took deep breaths.

"Mom, be still, or your eyeliner will be uneven," Talise fussed.

"Sorry, sweetie." Sandra slowly exhaled. What she had told Kelsi about hidden blessings was true, but her Raimond had been a long time coming.

From her dressing room tucked away on the mezzanine, she could hear the string quartet.

"I'm almost done."

Sandra dared not nod. Talise had already styled her hair into an updo with an explosion of cascading curls. Blush-colored pearls were tangled throughout the crown of her hair in a peek-a-boo fashion. Both her daughters-in-law teased her about her curves, so to test their theory Sandra purchased a dress on clearance from celebrity designer Lazaro Perez's collection online and prayed that it would fit or need little alteration, but it was perfect.

From her small waist up, Venise-lace covered her bodice and sleeves. A double row of blush pearls took the place of a zipper, and from the waist down, the same shade blush satin fitted her hips then flared out into a train that swished when she walked. That was the best part of watching models on the runway, their ability to ruffle the hems of their evening dresses in elegance. As soon as she slipped into her dress, her long-delayed fairytale would begin.

"Ready!"

Sandra opened her eyes and blinked at Talise's handiwork. She almost didn't recognize the glamorous woman in the mirror. "Ooh." She spun around so her granddaughters could see.

"Nani." They raced to her to touch her hair and face, but Talise intercepted. "No, girls." They resembled ballerinas in their flower girls dresses as Kami took their hands to lead them down the back staircase.

Left in the room with her two bridesmaids, Sandra needed Talise's help to get into her dress while Eva fanned herself. Her belly was swollen with Sandra's third grandchild.

"Don't you dare have that baby until after I'm married," Sandra warned, halfway serious. She loved her babies, but this was her day.

"I've put a request in," Eva said. "Two more weeks and I'm done."

"And I'll be just beginning," Talise said nonchalantly.

When the realization hit, Sandra screamed her delight, even Eva was up and at her side.

"Congratulations," Sandra and Eva said in unison as there was a knock at the door.

"Mom?" Ace asked on the other. "Ahh, we have a slight problem."

Sandra's heart leapt. *No, no. Lord, please, let this day be perfect.* She went to the door, but didn't open it. Eva and Talise were behind her. "What's wrong?"

Ace chuckled. "It appears your husband-to-be needs assistance."

"What kind?" Sandra stuttered, thinking broken leg, arm, heart attack…

"He needs help with his bow tie," Ace stated in a teasing tone.

All three of their sighs were audible.

"Is that all?" Talise fussed.

"I almost had this baby." Eva held her stomach.

Sandra cracked the door open and squinted at her son. "You're joking, right? Tell that man to do without."

"You can tell him yourself. He's out here."

"What!" Without thinking, she slammed the door in Ace's face. There was another knock. This time it was Raimond's voice. "Baby, please."

Eva finished buttoning her dress while Sandra checked her makeup when another knock came.

"I'm not leaving, wifey, until my demands are met," Raimond said.

"Seriously?" she shouted at the door. "Raimond Mayfield, we're not supposed to see each other yet." She shook her head. "The only way I would consider tying that bow is if you're blindfolded. Now, go away and meet me at the altar!" She giggled.

Sandra thought she had gotten rid of her groom, but five minutes later, there was another knock.

"Good grief. What now?" Talise asked.

This time, it was the photographer, wanting to capture the moment. "I already have a couple of shots of your son blindfolding him."

"I thought he was going to strangle me." Raimond snickered as he stepped into the room with his arms extending, feeling for something to steady him.

"He wouldn't, because both my sons know I waited so long for true love to come," she said softly.

"And your time is now," Talise whispered as she and Eva kissed Sandra on her cheek and slipped out, pushing Raimond aside.

The photographer followed and closed the door behind them.

Taking his hands, Sandra pulled him closer. "Are you sure you can't see me?" she asked.

"No." He rubbed her hands. "But you smell good. I love you," he whispered as the photographer snapped away.

"And I love you deeply too," she said, staring at him, beginning from his haircut, trimmed goatee, the fit of his tux, and even down to his shoes. Playing along, Raimond had been a good sport when he allowed Grandma BB to approve his Stacy Adams choice for the nuptials. So this is how handsome really looked when peering under a magnifying glass. However many more years God gave her on this earth, she wanted to spend them with Raimond Mayfield. And if she wanted to begin her life with this man, she better hurry. She quickly tied his bow tie, then adjusted it to perfection.

"Thank you, baby," he whispered.

"Always and forever."

Their photographer gave her a thumbs up and led her groom out of the room.

Alone, Sandra bowed her head and thanked God for her life's ups and downs. "Jesus, You have been faithful with Your blessings to me, even when I wasn't worthy. Thank You for preserving me for this man. Let our lives and love be a testimony to Your love…"

When the double knock came, Sandra quietly said amen. The two knocks meant both her sons were outside waiting to escort her to the altar.

Taking a deep breath, she opened the door to their stunned expressions.

"Ma." Kidd's jaw dropped. "Where have you been hiding…you?"

"I've been here all along," she said, slipping each arm through theirs. She swallowed. "I've been a mother for so long. Now, I'm ready to be Raimond's wife."

"She is one beautiful woman," Raimond's best man whispered beside him.

Raimond had his eyes locked on the second floor landing where his bride would grace any minute. Sandra's granddaughters had littered the runner with flowers, then stomped on them as they made their way to their mothers, the bridesmaids. "I promise to tell Sandra that until my last breath."

"Save that for your vows, man," Townsend said with a soft chuckle.

"I will." Raimond chanced a glance at his watch and

groaned. His bride was officially five minutes late. Although he was in perfect health, he prayed that her making him wait didn't give him a heart attack.

He had already scanned the number of guests in attendance. The layout had been strategic on Eva's part where everyone had a Birdseye view.

One guest—rather four of them—humbled him, his daughter, her husband, his grandson, and Kelsi's sister Lindsay. Their presence symbolized they were actively working on the bridge to reconciliation.

Raimond squinted at the second floor landing that was big enough to accommodate about twenty guests. They would be the first to see Sandra as she passed them as a queen making her way to the palace and they were her court.

When eyes widened and mouths dropped, Raimond braced himself and steadied his breathing.

Her two escorts or bodyguards, Kidd and Ace, seemed to block his view. Her train gave a glimpse of the beauty he was sure to see. When the trio turned at the top of the stairs and faced those below, Raimond's heart rate accelerated. Maybe he should have gotten a stress test.

Words couldn't begin to describe the sight to behold, except to say she was more beautiful than he could ever imagine.

Sandra and her sons waited as the photographer snapped away.

How many pictures did the man need? Raimond wanted to know. *Come on.*

Finally, Sandra began her descent down the twenty-two steps—he had counted them and Raimond calculated forty seconds from the top to the bottom.

Elegant, regal, stunning, and youthful were a few words to describe his bride as his eyes captured hers. Everything around him blurred.

They were taking too long to bring her, so Raimond marched to the bottom stair and reached out his hand to speed them along. Sandra closed her eyes as she received a kiss on each cheek from Kidd, then Ace.

"Be happy," Kidd whispered to Sandra, then turned and mouthed to him, "Or you won't."

Not today, Raimond said to himself as he ignored Kidd and shook Ace's hand and then Kidd's before taking Sandra's and carefully guiding her down the remaining stairs. "If I knew you looked this beautiful, I would have peeped under that blindfold." Sandra blushed. "You'll always be my dream come true."

Her beauty was timeless with an enchanting neckline that made him want to tickle with kisses. Her perfume was teasing, but it was the sleek dress that seemed to accent every perfect curve God had preserved until this day. He blinked as the minister cleared his throat.

With Sandra's hand securely on his arm, Raimond walked to him. The pastor seemed amused as Raimond wiped at the beads of perspiration on his forehead.

"Dearly Beloved, we are gathered together here in the sight of God and in the face of this company to join together this man and this woman in holy matrimony, which is honorable among all men. This covenant is not to be entered into unadvisedly or lightly, but reverently, discreetly, advisedly, and solemnly. If any person can show just cause why this man and this woman may not be joined together, let them speak now or forever hold their peace." He searched the audience. "I understand you have written your own vows. Raimond, you may go first."

Gathering Sandra's hands in his, Raimond lifted them to his lips. When he brushed a kiss on her knuckles, she shivered to his delight. "Sandra Nicholson, love is patient, love is kind, but love is incomplete without you. I promise you my faithfulness…"

When Raimond finished, he kissed her knuckles again and lowered her hands, but didn't let go.

"Sandra." The pastor nodded.

Her eyes sparkled. "Raimond Mayfield, I thought love had passed me by until you stopped traffic to get my attention." They shared a chuckle and so did others who knew their story. "I'm addicted to your goal to love me. I promise to pray for you and be one with you in thoughts, goals, and desire. I promise to honor you as my husband and respect and submit to you as you follow Christ…"

The pastor smiled. "By the power of God invested in me, the Pentecostal Assemblies of the World and the state of Missouri, I now pronounce you Mr. And Mrs. Raimond Mayfield. What the Lord has joined together from the beginning of time, let no demon, whether in the form of a man or woman, come between you to destroy. In Jesus' name. Amen.

Raimond touched her chin and coaxed her to meet his waiting lips. Once she did, he swallowed her up in his arms and teased her with the promises of passions to come.

Sparks ignited the moment they touched. Only the catcalls, whistles, applause tamed his indulgence. Turning around, the cameras flashed as he grinned.

He had a wife now to have and to hold from that day forward until his last breath.

Epilogue

"Hmmm, you smell good, Mrs. Mayfield," Raimond mumbled as he nibbled on her neck as they lounged on the sofa. A rainy weekend gave them the perfect excuse to stay inside.

Sandra giggled at his naughtiness, making her blissfully happy. Glancing over her shoulder and staring into her husband's brown eyes, she rubbed his smooth jaw. "For you," she whispered and he rewarded her with a lingering kiss.

Raimond never rushed his affections, which gave her time to experience every moment in slow motion. This man had been a love worth waiting for. Sandra almost purred from contentment as she snuggled deeper under his arms. Together they admired the photos in their wedding albums, the evidence that she was indeed a married woman, finally. Her eyes watered when realization hit that she belonged to someone. Besides being a mother, mother-in-law, and Nani, she had been officially a wife one month and counting.

Time had stopped as the camera's lens captured more than the color-scheme, flowers, or backdrop. The photographer had archived their love for years to come. The close-ups, especially of Raimond, revealed the wonderment in his eyes of his love for her. From the kiss to seal their vows, to the hint of mischief as he gathered her in his arms for their first dance, to Raimond's gentle coaxing to feed her a slice of their wedding cake. The day had truly been perfect, surreal, and sensual. Even without the pictures and the keepsakes displayed in her curio cabinet, Sandra had stored up memories to savor at a moment's notice.

One of her favorites of the day had been the African American figurine where the groom lifted the bride off her feet. That image conveyed how Raimond made her feel— young, carefree, and in love.

In the cocoon of her husband's arms, Sandra's mind drifted. When he whispered sweet scenarios in her ear, Sandra blushed and playfully nudged him back. "Behave, husband." She pecked his pouty lips. "Come on. For days I've been trying to finish looking through our wedding album, but you've been distracting me. Now stop it," she feigned a stern warning.

He moaned and twisted his mouth in disappointed. "All right, I'll behave, but trust me, when you turn to the last page, you're mine for the rest of the evening, Mrs. Mayfield."

After sealing the deal with a few kisses, they returned to the pictures; Raimond with too much gusto while Sandra wanted to savor the memories.

"Look at my—our—babies." Laughing, Sandra had to get used to sharing everything with him. There was no longer his or hers, but *ours*. She couldn't believe Kennedy and Lauren's antics as they stomped on the petals they had littered on the runner as flower girls.

"You should've seen them do it." Raimond chuckled. "Pictures don't tell it all. On the next trip back to Boston, we should take the girls to the Black Doll Museum in Mansfield, Massachusetts. I think they would enjoy that."

How thoughtful. "I didn't even know there was one so close to me when I lived there."

Raimond rubbed a kiss into her hair. "Look at my—our other babies," he repeated while his eyes gazed at the picture of Kelsi holding Baby Stephan. "When our grandchildren get older, we'll do a road trip to Chicago and visit the Bronzville's Children Museum."

Their grandchildren now included Sandra's newest grandchild, Kevin Jamieson Junior. It served her son right for Eva to insist on naming their son after him. But she had every confidence in God that Kidd would be a great role model to Little Kidd as the family had started to call him.

"We never can start too early for them to learn about their proud heritage," Raimond chatted away, pulling her mind back to the present.

As she turned the page, they both laughed uncontrollably.

"I don't care what anybody says." He pointed. "That woman takes weird to another level."

"She wouldn't be Grandma BB, if she didn't. I've learned not to question anything with her."

"But men's shoes to a wedding, babe?"

"Hey, she knows how to color coordinate. She wore two-tone burgundy ones to Ace and Talise's wedding when she was escorted down the aisle as the honorary Jamieson granny." She tapped her finger on the picture. "She's a fashionista. Everyone is praying that one of these days, she'll stop playing with God and get in a committed relationship with Him. It looks like she is comparing her shoes with another guest's."

"That's Mr. Moore. He had been a big supporter of the black museum before I opened. He's a talking Wikipedia of Black history and he donated several items too. I wonder how old she really is?"

Before Raimond could say more, Sandra reached for their bowl of forgotten grapes. She fed Raimond first, then popped one into her mouth. "Probably in her nineties, but only social security knows for sure."

They continued admiring the lovely snapshots. She smiled when she came to a picture of Kelsi's brother, Tyler, and Raimond's confidant, Townsend. Both were vying for Queen Jamieson's attention. Studying Queen's body language, Sandra decided it would be a tossup on who would capture her affections. Either way, one would have to face Kidd's interrogation Sandra was sure.

Raimond shook his head and grunted. "Townsend's going to have to step up his game if he wants that woman. Queen Jamieson doesn't look like she takes any prisoners."

"She doesn't." Sandra flipped through more pages, then turned back. "This seems more interesting."

"A picture is worth a thousand words," Raimond mumbled as they scrutinized Dace and Lindsay in some type of animated conversation. Whatever the topic was, they had some fierce expressions.

"I would've liked to be a fly on the wall to hear them. Kelsi's siblings really resemble her."

He nodded and shifted his body to stretch. "No one would ever know that they're half-brother and sisters."

"Or biracial children of a white father." Ivy had some strong genes, but Sandra had seen glimpses of Raimond in his daughter's expressions.

"He's not white, honey. He's light enough that he and his family could've passed for white, but that's another chapter in somebody else's story, Mrs. Mayfield," her husband said in a baritone voice that made her float. "Last page." He closed the album and stood. "Let's make some of our own memories hidden from the camera."

He guided Sandra to her feet, then scooped her up in his arms, flexing his biceps. "I've gotcha, babe."

And Sandra believed him, not just her weight, but her heart. If the Lord willed, she and Raimond might make that forty-year wedding anniversary.

A Note

from the Author

Thanks so much for waiting for Sandra's story. She first appeared in *Guilty by Association* (Kidd and Eva's story), then *The Guilt Trip* (Ace and Talise's story).

She was a special lady who had turned her life around. Many of you felt she deserved a happy ending and I hope I gave you one.

In case you didn't read *Sandra Nicholson's Back Story*, you can download it and get the scoop on how she fell hard for Samuel Jamieson.

A sequel is never a given when I write my books, but as I developed Lindsay's character, Kelsi's younger sister, I thought she needed to have a love of her own. Dace, Raimond's museum sculptor was a good candidate, then something happened at Raimond and Sandra's wedding, and their attraction ended before it took off. Hmmm, I'm sure you want to know what irked Lindsay.

Watch out for her story next. What title would you

give Lindsay's story? Email your suggestion at authorpatsimmons.net and enter to win bragging right for the title, a mention in the book and an autograph copy.

Sign up for my newsletter, so you'll be the first to know when I come up with a title. My website is www.patsimmons.net.

Also, if you want to take a look at some of the old documents that Raimond had on display in his museum please visit me on Pinterest.com/patsimmonsbooks and click on *The Confession* Board where the pictures truly tell the story.

And one more thing, the house I modeled The Heritage House Museum after does exist. It was my grandmother's old mansion-size house that was in need of major repairs when I sold it for little to nothing. The owner renovated it into a Bed and Breakfast. I'm not sure if it is still operating today.

Book Club Questions

1. Discuss whether Ivy made the right decision to give Raimond Kelsi's number before talking to her daughter.

2. Discuss Sandra's determination to confess to Samuel's first wife.

3. Kidd found a kindred spirit with Kelsi at the museum's grand opening. Talk about the realism of their conversation.

4. Was Sandra sympathetic to Raimond's plight with reconciling his daughter?

5. Name the black history headlines outlined in this story you've heard in school or at home.

6. Have you confessed your sins to Jesus? Discuss whether Raimond gave Sandra good advice about who to confess your past to.

If you've enjoyed Sandra and Raimond's story, please consider posting a review, then signing up for my monthly newsletter at authorpatsimmons@gmail.com.

About the Author

Pat is the multi-published author of several single titles and eBook novellas, and is a two-time recipient of the Emma Rodgers Award for Best Inspirational Romance. She has been a featured speaker and workshop presenter at various venues across the country.

As a self-proclaimed genealogy sleuth, Pat is passionate about researching her ancestors and then casting them in starring roles in her novels. She describes the evidence of the gift of the Holy Ghost as an amazing, unforgettable, life-altering experience. God is the Author who advances the stories she writes.

Pat is currently overseeing the media publicity for the annual RT Booklovers Conventions. She has a B.S. in mass communications from Emerson College in Boston, Massachusetts.

Pat converted her sofa-strapped, sports fanatic husband into an amateur travel agent, untrained bodyguard, GPS-guided chauffeur, and administrative assistant who is constantly on probation. They have a son and a daughter.

Read more about Pat and her books by visiting www.patsimmons.net or on social media.

Other Christian Titles Include

The Guilty series
Book I: *Guilty of Love*
Book II: *Not Guilty of Love*
Book III: *Still Guilty*
Book IV: *The Acquittal*

The Jamieson Legacy
Book I: *Guilty by Association*
Book II: *The Guilt Trip*
Book III: *Free from Guilt*
Book IV: *The Confession*

The Carmen Sisters
Book I: *No Easy Catch*
Book II: *In Defense of Love*
Book III: *Redeeming Heart*
Book IV: *Driven to Be Loved*

Love at the Crossroads
Book I: *Stopping Traffic*
Book II: *A Baby for Christmas*
Book III: *The Keepsake*
Book IV: *What God Has for Me*

Making Love Work, a theme anthology
Book I: *Love at Work*
Book II: *Words of Love*
Book III: *A Mother's Love*

Single titles
Crowning Glory
Talk to Me
Her Dress (novella)

Holiday titles
Love for the Holidays
(Three Christian novellas)
A Christian Christmas
A Christian Easter
A Christian Father's Day
A Woman After David's Heart
(Valentine's Day)
Christmas Greetings
A Noelle for Nathan

LOVE AT THE CROSSROADS SERIES

—STOPPING TRAFFIC—

Candace Clark has a phobia about crossing the street. As fate would have it, her daughter's principal assigns her to crossing guard duties as part of the school's parent participation program. Candace begrudgingly accepts her stop sign and safety vest, then reports to her designated crosswalk. She's determined to overcome her fears, and God opens the door for a blessing, and Royce Kavanaugh enters into her life, a firefighter built to rescue any damsel in distress.

—A BABY FOR CHRISTMAS—

Yes, diamonds are a girl's best friend, but in Solae Wyatt-Palmer's case, she desires something more valuable. Captain Hershel Kavanaugh is a divorcee and the father of two adorable little boys. Solae has never been married and longs to be a mother. Although Hershel showers her with expensive gifts, his hesitation about proposing causes Solae to walk and never look back. As the holidays approach, Hershel must convince Solae that she has everything he could ever want for Christmas.

—THE KEEPSAKE—

Until death us do part... Desiree "Desi" Bishop is devastated when she learns of her husband's affair. God knew she didn't get married only to one day have to stand before a judge and file for a divorce. But Desi wants out no matter how much her heart says to forgive Michael. She sees God's one acceptable reason for a divorce as the only opt-out clause in her marriage. Michael Bishop is a repenting man who loves his wife. If only...he had paid attention to the red flags God sent to keep him from falling into the devil's snares. Although God's forgives instantly, Desi's forgiveness is moving as a snail's pace. After all the tears have been shed and forgiveness granted and received, the couple learns that some marriages are worth keeping.

—WHAT GOD HAS FOR ME—

Pregnant Halcyon Holland is leaving her live-in boyfriend, taking their daughter with her. When her ex doesn't reconcile their relationship, Halcyon begins to second-guess whether or not she compromised her chance for a happily ever after. But Zachary Bishop has had his eye on Halcyon for a long time. Without a ring on her finger, Zachary prays that she will come to her senses and not only leave Scott, but come back to God. What one man doesn't cherish, Zach is ready to treasure. Not deterred by Halcyon's broken spirit, Zachary is on a mission to offer her a second chance at love that she can't refuse. And as far as her adorable children are concerned, Zachary's love is unconditional for a ready-made family. Halcyon will soon learn that her past circumstances won't hinder the Lord's blessings, because what God has for her, is for her

LOVE FOR THE HOLIDAYS SERIES

—A CHRISTIAN CHRISTMAS—

Christmas will never be the same for Joy Knight if Christian Andersen has his way. Christian and his family are busy making sure the Lord's blessings are distributed to those less fortunate by Christmas day. Joy is playing the hand that life dealt her, rearing four children in a home that is on the brink of foreclosure. She's not looking for a handout when Christian Andersen rescues her in the checkout line. Can time spent with him turn Joy's attention from her financial woes to the real meaning of Christmas and true love?

—A CHRISTIAN EASTER—

How to celebrate Easter becomes a balancing act for Christian and Joy Andersen and their four children. Chocolate bunnies, colorful stuffed baskets and flashy fashion shows are their competition. Despite the enticements, Christian refuses to succumb without a fight. And it becomes a tug of war when his recently adopted ten year-old daughter, Bethani, wants to participate in her friend's Easter tradition. Christian hopes he has instilled Proverbs

22:6, into the children's heart in the short time of being their dad.

—A CHRISTIAN FATHER'S DAY—

Three fathers, one Father's Day and four children. Will the real dad, please stand up. It's never too late to be a father—or is it? Christian Andersen was looking forward to spending his first Father's day with his adopted children—all four of them. But Father's day becomes more complicated than Christian or Joy ever imagined. Christian finds himself faced with living up to his name when things don't go his way to enjoy an idyllic once a year celebration. But he depends on God to guide him through the journey.

—A WOMAN AFTER DAVID'S HEART—

David Andersen doesn't want a woman to get any ideas that a wedding ring was forthcoming before he got a chance to know her if their first date is on Valentine's Day. So he has no choice but to wait until the whole Valentine's Day hoopla was over, then he would make his move on a sister in his church he can't take his eyes off of. For the past two years and counting, Valerie Hart hasn't been the recipient of a romantic

Valentine's Day dinner invitation. To fill the void, Valerie keeps herself busy with God's business, hoping the Lord will send her perfect mate soon.

—CHRISTMAS GREETINGS—

For Saige Carter, Christmas wouldn't be complete without family and friends to share in the traditions they've created together. Plus, Saige is extra excited about her line of Christmas greeting cards hitting store shelves, but when she gets devastating news around the holidays, she wonders if she'll ever look at Christmas the same again.

Daniel Washington is no Scrooge, but he'd rather skip the holidays altogether than spend them with his estranged family. After one too many arguments around the dinner table one year, Daniel had enough and walked away from the drama. When Daniel reads one of Saige's greeting cards, he's unsure if the words inside are enough to erase the pain and bring about forgiveness.

MAKING LOVE WORK SERIES

—A MOTHER'S LOVE—

Jillian Carter became a teenage mother when she confused love for lust one summer. Despite the sins of her past, Jesus forgave her and blessed her to be the best Christian example for Shana. Jillian is not looking forward to becoming an empty-nester at thirty-nine. The old adage, she's not losing a daughter, but gaining a son-in-law is not comforting as she braces for a lonely life ahead. Shana's biological father breezes back into their lives as a redeemed man and practicing Christian. Not only is Alex still good-looking, but he's willing to right the wrong he's done in the past. The widower father of the groom, Dr. Dexter Harris, has set his sights on Jillian and he's willing to pull out all the stops to woo her. Now the choice is hers. Who will be the next mother's love?

—LOVE AT WORK—

How do two people go undercover to hide an office romance in a busy television newsroom? In plain sight, of course. Desiree King is an assignment editor at KDPX-TV in St. Louis, MO. She dispatches a team to wherever breaking news happens. When it comes to dating a fellow coworker, she refuses to cross that professional line. Award-winning investigative reporter Brooke Mitchell makes life challenging for Desiree with his thoughtful gestures, sweet notes, and support. He tries to convince Desiree that as Christians, they could show coworkers how to blend their personal and private lives without compromising their morals.

—WORDS OF LOVE—

Simone French was smitten with a love letter. Not a text, email, or Facebook post, but a love letter sent through snail mail. The prose wasn't the corny roses-are-red-and-violets-are-blue stuff. The first letter contained short accolades for a job well done. Soon after, the missives were filled with passionate words from a man who confessed the hidden secrets of his soul. He revealed his unspoken weaknesses, listed his uncompromising desires, and unapologetically noted his subtle strengths. Yes, Rice Taylor was ready to surrender to love. Whew. Closing her eyes, Simone inhaled the faint lingering smell of roses on the beige plain stationery. She had a testimony. If anyone would listen, she would proclaim that love was truly blind.

—MY TESTIMONY:
IF I SHOULD DIE BEFORE I WAKE—

It is of the LORD's mercies that we are not consumed, because His compassions fail not. They are new every morning, great is Thy faithfulness. Lamentations 3:22-23, God's mercies are sure; His promises are fulfilled; but a dawn of a new morning is God' grace. If you need a testimony about God's grace, then IF I SHOULD DIE BEFORE I WAKE will encourage your soul. Nothing happens in our lives by chance. If you need a miracle, God's got that too. Trust Him. Has it been a while since you've had a testimony? Increase your prayer life, build your faith and walk in victory because without a test, there is no testimony.

The Guilty Series

Kick Off

GUILTY OF LOVE

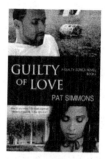

When do you know the most important decision of your life is the right one?

Reaping the seeds from what she's sown; Cheney Reynolds moves into a historic neighborhood in Ferguson, Missouri, and becomes a reclusive. Her first neighbor, the incomparable Mrs. Beatrice Tilley Beacon aka Grandma BB, is an opinionated childless widow. Then there is Parke Kokumuo Jamison VI, a direct descendant of a royal African tribe. He learned his family ancestry, African history, and lineage preservation before he could count. Unwittingly, they are drawn to each other, but it takes Christ to weave their lives into a spiritual bliss while He exonerates their past indiscretions.

—NOT GUILTY OF LOVE—

One man, one woman, one God and one big problem. Malcolm Jamieson wasn't the man who got away, but the man God instructed Hallison Dinkins to set free. Instead of their explosive love affair leading them to the wedding altar, God diverted Hallison to the prayer altar.

Malcolm was convinced that his woman had loss her mind to break off their engagement. Didn't Hallison know that

Malcolm, a tenth generation descendant of a royal African tribe, couldn't be replaced? Once Malcolm concedes that their relationship can't be savaged, he issues Hallison his own edict, "If we're meant to be with each other, we'll find our way back. If not, that means that there's a love stronger than what we had." Someone has to retreat, and God never loses a battle.

—STILL GUILTY—

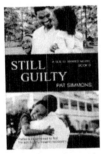

Cheney Reynolds Jamieson made a choice years ago that is now shaping her future and the future of the men she loves. A botched abortion left her unable to carry a baby to term, and her husband, Parke K. Jamison VI, is expected to produce heirs. With a wife who cannot give him a child, Parke vows to find and get custody of his illegitimate son by any means necessary. Meanwhile, Cheney's twin brother, Rainey, struggles with his anger over his ex-girlfriend's actions that haunt him, and their father, Dr. Roland Reynolds, fights to keep an old secret in the past.

THE GUILTY PARTIES SERIES

—*THE ACQUITTAL*—

Two worlds apart, but their hearts dance to the same African drum beat. On a professional level, Dr. Rainey Reynolds is a competent, highly sought-after orthodontist. Inwardly, he needs to be set free from the chaos of revelations that make him question if happiness is obtainable. To get away from the drama, Rainey is willing to leave the country under the guise of a mission trip with Dentist Without Borders. Will changing his surroundings really change him? Ghanaian beauty Josephine Abena Yaa Amoah returns to Africa after completing her studies in America. She prays for Rainey's surrender to Christ in order for God to acquit him of his self-inflicted mental torture. In the Motherland of Ghana, Africa, Rainey not only visits the places of his ancestors, will he embrace the liberty that Christ's Blood really does set every man free.

—THE CONFESSION—

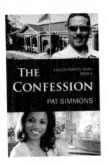

Sandra Nicholson, Kidd and Ace Jamieson's mother is on the threshold of happiness, but Kidd believes no man is good enough for his mother, especially if her love interest could be a man just like his absentee father.

THE JAMIESON LEGACY SERIES

—GUILTY BY ASSOCIATION—

How important is a name? To the St. Louis Jamiesons who are tenth generation descendants of a royal African tribe—everything. To the Boston Jamiesons whose father never married their mother—there is no loyalty or legacy. Kidd Jamieson suffers from the "angry" male syndrome because his father was an absent in the home, but insisted his two sons carry his last name. It takes an old woman who mingles genealogy truths and Bible verses together for Kidd to realize his worth as a strong black man. He learns it's not his association with the name that identifies him, but the man he becomes that defines him.

—THE GUILT TRIP—

Aaron "Ace" Jamieson is living a carefree life. He's good-looking, respectable when he's in the mood, but his weakness is women. If a woman tries to ambush him with a pregnancy, he takes off in the other direction. It's a lesson learned from his absentee father that responsibility is optional. Talise Rogers has a bright future ahead of her. She's pretty and has no problem catching a man's eye, which is exactly what she does with Ace. Trapping Ace Jamieson is the furthest thing from Taleigh's mind when she learns she pregnant and Ace rejects her. "I want nothing from you Ace, not even your name." And Talise meant it.

—*FREE FROM GUILT*—

It's salvation round-up time and Cameron Jamieson's name is on God's hit list.

Although his brothers and cousins embraced God—thanks to the women in their lives—the two-degreed MIT graduate isn't going to let any woman take him down that path without a fight. He's satisfied with his career, social calendar, and good genes. But God uses a beautiful messenger, Gabrielle Dupree, to show him that he's in a spiritual deficit. Cameron learns the hard way that man's wisdom is like foolishness to God. For every philosophical argument he throws her way, Gabrielle exposes him to scriptures that makes him question his worldly knowledge.

THE CARMEN SISTERS SERIES

—NO EASY CATCH—

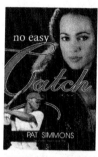

Shae Carmen discovered that her boyfriend was not only married, but on the verge of reconciling with his estranged wife. Humiliated, Shae begins to second guess herself as why she didn't see the signs that he was nothing more than a devil's decoy masquerading as a devout Christian man. St. Louis Outfielder Rahn Maxwell finds himself a victim of an attempted carjacking. The Lord guides him out of harms' way by opening the gunmen's eyes to Rahn's identity and they direct him out of their ambush! When the news media gets wind of what happened with the baseball player, Shae's television station lands an exclusive interview. Just when Shae lets her guard down, she is faced with another scandal that rocks her world. This time the stakes are higher. Not only is her heart on the line, so is her professional credibility.

—IN DEFENSE OF LOVE—

Lately, nothing in Garrett Nash's life has made sense. When two people close to the U.S. Marshal wrong him deeply, Garrett expects God to remove them from his life. Instead, the Lord relocates Garrett to another city to start over, as if he were the offender instead of the victim.

Criminal attorney Shari Carmen is comfortable in her own skin—most of the time. Being a "dark and lovely" African-American sister has its challenges, especially when it comes to relationships. While playing tenor saxophone at an anniversary party, she grabs the attention of Garrett Nash. And as God draws them closer together, He makes another request of Garrett, one to which it will prove far more difficult to say "Yes, Lord."

—REDEEMING HEART—

Landon Thomas brings a new definition to the word "prodigal," as in prodigal son, brother or anything else imaginable. It's a good thing that God's love covers a multitude of sins, but He isn't letting Landon off easy. His journey from riches to rags proves to be humbling and a lesson well learned.

Real Estate Agent Octavia Winston is a woman on a mission, whether it's God's or hers professionally. One thing is for certain, she's not about to compromise when it comes to a Christian mate, so why did God send a homeless man to steal her heart?

Minister Rossi Tolliver (Crowning Glory) knows how to minister to God's lost sheep and through God's redemption, the game changes for Landon and Octavia.

—DRIVEN TO BE LOVED—

On the surface, Brecee Carmen has nothing in common with Adrian Cole. She is a pediatrician certified in trauma care; he is a transportation problem–solver for a luxury car dealership (a.k.a., a car salesman). Neither one of them is sure that they're compatible. To complicate matters, Brecee is the sole unattached Carmen daughter when it seems as though everyone else around her—family and friends—is finding love. Through a series of discoveries, Adrian and Brecee learn that things don't always happen by coincidence. Generational forces are at work, keeping promises, protecting family members, and perhaps even drawing Adrian back to the church he had strayed from. Is it possible that God has been playing matchmaker all along?

SINGLE TITLES

—CROWNING GLORY—

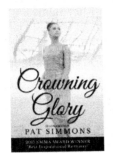

Cinderella had a prince; Karyn Wallace has a King.

While Karyn served four years in prison for an unthinkable crime, she embraced salvation through Crowns for Christ outreach ministry. After her release, Karyn stays strong and confident, despite the stigma society places on ex-offenders. Since Christ strengthens the underdog, Karyn refuses to sway away from the scripture, "He who the Son has set free is free indeed."

Levi Tolliver is steadfast there is a price to pay for every sin committed, especially after the untimely death of his wife during a robbery. Then Karyn enters Levi's life. He is enthralled not only with her beauty, but her sweet spirit until he learns about her incarceration. If Levi can accept that Christ paid Karyn's debt in full, then a treasure awaits him.

—TALK TO ME—

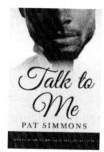

Despite being deaf as a result of a fireworks explosion, CEO of a St. Louis non-profit company, Noel Richardson, expertly navigates the hearing world. What some view as a disability, Noel views as a challenge—his lack of hearing has never held him back.

It also helps that he has great looks, numerous university degrees, and full bank accounts. But those assets don't define him as a man who longs for the right woman in his life.

Deciding to visit a church service, Noel is blind-sided by the most beautiful and graceful Deaf interpreter he's ever seen. Mackenzie Norton challenges him on every level through words and signing, but as their love grows, their faith is tested.

When their church holds a yearly revival, they witness the healing power of God in others. Mackenzie has faith to believe that Noel can also get in on the blessing. Since faith comes by hearing, whose voice does Noel hear in his heart, Mackenzie or God's?

—HER DRESS—

Sometimes a woman just wants to splurge on something new, especially when she's about to attend an event with movers and shakers. Find out what happens when Pepper Trudeau is all dressed up and goes to the ball, but another woman is modeling the same attire. At first, Pepper is embarrassed, then the night gets interesting when she meets Drake Logan. Her Dress is a romantic novella about the all too common occurrence—two women shopping at the same place. Maybe having the same taste isn't all bad. Sometimes a good dress is all you need to meet the man of your dreams.

Check out my fellow Christian fiction authors writing about
faith, family and love
with African-American characters.
You won't be disappointed!

www.blackchristianreads.com

CPSIA information can be obtained
at www.ICGtesting.com
Printed in the USA
LVOW13s1427070417
530034LV00007B/191/P